LEADING

KYLIE GILMORE

What are the odds two people fall in love?

1

———

Galena

I'm not a romantic. As a biostatistician, I calculate the odds of success before moving forward with any plan. Today, my elopement wedding day, has actually been very well planned. I would never spontaneously elope. *Horror*.

"Stunning," Paige says as she does the clasp on a tiny pearl necklace for me. She's the innkeeper of the Inn at Lovers' Lane, where I'm eloping in an outdoor ceremony on a Saturday in June.

"Thank you." My voice sounds soft as if coming from a great distance. I'm having a weird out-of-body experience watching myself get ready in an upstairs guest room at the inn. Somehow none of this feels real. My mind wanders in a fuzzy, dreamlike state as I struggle to return to my usual logical self.

Everything is perfect—the weather, my gown, my future marriage. There's no reason at all to be concerned.

Two months ago, Kevin and I bought a house together here in Summerdale, New York. Marriage was the next logical step. We've been together for two years and two months, and two years of that time was spent living together, first in an apartment and then a house. I've dreamed of living in a house my entire life. Everything is just how I want it to be. I review the facts once more:

Kevin and I are both busy professionals.

An elopement saves time and money.

Odds are for a successful future together.

Kevin's a dedicated research scientist whom I have a lot of respect for. He asks little of me, as I do of him. Like I said, perfectly compatible. A dating app even thought so, which is how we met.

I fluff the layers of tulle at the bottom of my dream wedding gown. It's a full-length white dress with a V-neck, thin shoulder straps, beaded waist, and an overlay of floral lace. I can't believe it was so affordable too. It was meant to be, just like my marriage. That cheers me a bit.

Maybe I'm not quite myself because *Leisure Travel* magazine is here to cover the event. I've never been one to grab the spotlight, preferring to be in the background, thinking deeply about problems and calculating the odds of successful solutions. That's what I do at work, analyze the data for new drugs and medical treatments at a pharmaceutical company.

Anyway, the inn prides itself on elopement weddings. The timing worked out, and if I'm being honest, there's some family tension about Kevin, which is why I didn't tell anyone in my family about today's wedding except my grandparents who live in Las Vegas, where we plan to honeymoon. I know that sounds bad, but in my traditional family, it's a major sin to live together before marriage.

My parents and grandparents have mostly pretended Kevin doesn't exist. They've never met him, and he hasn't cared about being left out of family events. I get a Christmas card every year from my parents, addressed only to me. But all that will change with our marriage, right? They'll *have* to acknowledge his place in my life.

Only my sister, Izzy, has met him, and she didn't like him, though she could never say exactly why. I wipe sweat from my brow, my heart suddenly racing. I didn't invite my only sister, my closest best friend to my wedding. I wanted to invite her, but I was afraid she'd object.

It's just me, Kevin, and the magazine people. Adrenaline surges through me, and I fight the urge to run. What is wrong with me today? Kayla is here, a close friend of mine. Her older sisters run the inn. She's claimed me as an honorary sister because, as she says, we're practically twins—both biostatisticians at the same company, both the youngest in our family and the smartest. Ha.

I take a slow deep breath. I've done the math. This marriage makes perfect sense. And I'm fine with Kevin not wanting kids. I have Izzy's girls, my beloved nieces. I try to think of something great about being child-free, like we could take off at a moment's notice to Tahiti, though we rarely take time off work.

"Here." Paige hands me a bridal bouquet of pale pink roses with baby's breath. She's a little brusque because she's stressed about the *Leisure Travel* article going well, as well as noticeably pregnant.

I stare at the flowers, my eyes hot and stinging with tears. I'm sure my family will grow to love Kevin just like I did. The alternative is too horrible to think about.

"No crying until after the ceremony," Paige says sternly. "We didn't hire a makeup artist so you could ruin your make-up." She gives my shoulder a squeeze and turns me to face the full-length mirror. "Look at this beautiful bride."

I blink a few times, barely recognizing myself. My shoulder-length dark brown hair is styled so it falls in soft waves with no hint of frizz. I'm wearing contacts instead of my usual black-framed glasses, and my olive skin glows. And the gown, ooh, the gown, it has just the right amount of elegance, romantic even. Perfect for an outdoor summer ceremony. I ordered it online with Paige's approval since it needs to look good in glossy magazine pictures.

Surely the magazine feature will up the cool factor with my family and balance out the uncool fact of marrying secretly. At least we'll be married instead of just living together. That should score major points with them.

"Now let's get you into those heels," Paige says.

She fetches the gold block heels from a corner of the room. I slip off my white sneakers and slide into the heels.

"I've been practicing with these," I tell her.

"Good. Last thing we want is our bride face-planting halfway down the aisle." She laughs.

I smile, though I can picture that happening so clearly I can't quite manage to laugh along. Not saying I'm a klutz. Just that sometimes I'm so lost in thought I lose track of my surroundings.

Kayla walks in. "Oh, Galena, you look so beautiful!" She hugs me. Kayla is the nicer, sweeter version of her older sister Paige. They look similar with brown hair and light brown eyes.

"Hey, careful not to wrinkle her gown!" Paige protests.

Kayla straightens out a tulle layer for me. "Sorry I missed the dressing part, but I wanted to make sure all the details were perfect outside. We just finished up. And your groom is here!"

My stomach does a little flip.

"Great," I say hoarsely. Of course Kevin's here. He was too busy with work to be involved in any of the elopement planning or meeting with the *Leisure Travel* people ahead of time, but he wouldn't miss his own wedding.

I go to the window and take in the backyard, where a white wedding pergola awaits in the distance, decorated with red roses and greenery. There's a white runner leading to it. A single row of chairs is set up for the reporter, photographer, and the sisters running the show at the inn. It looks pretty but empty. Not like I had some great fantasy about my wedding day. I guess I just thought I'd feel more, be swept up in the momentous occasion. Instead, I feel deflated.

The mayor of Summerdale strides over to the pergola in a navy suit. He's the wedding officiant. Levi Appleton. He's young for a mayor, late twenties I'm guessing, with brown hair on the longish side and a beard. He suddenly looks up, meeting my eyes. A jolt hits me just like the last time our eyes met, and the time before that. He has that effect on me. I can't explain it.

I first met him two months ago here at the inn for the meeting with the magazine people and had a strange experience. Our gazes locked, sending a jolt through me, my mind going blank. Very unlike me to have a jolt or a blank mind. I'm always thinking. Afterward, Kayla filled me in on him. She knows him well since he's her next-door neighbor and good friends with her husband. She says he's a great guy, twice elected mayor. Her sisters sang his praises too. I figured the strange jolt I got when our eyes met was due to his natural charisma. My theory was that he had a big effect on everyone the first time they met him, sort of like meeting a celebrity or rock star with all their charisma, which could explain why he's a popular mayor.

But the strange experiences continued every time I ran into him around town while I was running errands. He was always warm and friendly, never too friendly, definitely not flirting, yet when our eyes met, a jolt went through me, followed by a rush of heat. It made no sense. Why would this happen after a first meeting with nothing more than friendly warm smiles? Super charisma? Maybe he has that effect on all women, though it's hard to tell because I haven't seen him with any single women to judge accurately.

I tear my gaze away and spy Kevin's blond head fixated on his phone like usual over by a white tent in the side yard set up for a small reception with champagne and appetizers.

Brooke bursts into the room. She's the middle sister between Paige and Kayla, and co-owner of the inn. "How's it going? Everyone ready?"

"All good here," Paige says.

Brooke approaches me, her green eyes full of concern. "You doing okay, Galena? You look a little, uh, unwell."

All three sisters stare at me.

I let out a breath. "I'm just a little nervous about the magazine people."

"Focus on your groom," Paige orders. "This is your special day. They've promised to be as unobtrusive as possible."

I nod even as sweat runs down my spine. Jittery nerves have me slowly moving toward the bed and sitting down. "Can I have a few minutes to myself?"

"Of course!" Paige says, hustling her sisters out of the room.

"You've got this!" Kayla calls on her way out.

I lift a hand in acknowledgment. As soon as they leave, I pick up my purse from the nightstand and retrieve my phone. I need to text my sister. I'd call, but my nieces, ages four and six, make it hard for her to talk on the phone. She can almost always send off a quick text. Just need to check in, see how everyone's doing.

Oh, there's a text from Kevin. He didn't want to see me in my wedding gown until the ceremony for the "wow" factor, but he still took the time to text. That's nice. I tap over to it.

Kevin: *I can't do this. The wedding's off. Can you let the inn staff know?*

2

———

My jaw gapes as the words blur in front of my eyes. The phone clatters to the floor from my limp hand, my entire body goes cold, and I collapse backward on the bed. The room fades from view, sounds coming at me from a great distance.

Nonsense, nonsensical, no sense at all.

Floating away, away, away.

Time passes for long numb moments…until a familiar feminine voice speaks urgently by my ear; pressure on my shoulders and then a shake.

Kayla's face hovers over mine, her hands on my shoulders. "What happened? Are you okay?"

I stare at her, shock giving way to harsh reality. My lungs constrict, making it hard to breathe. My limbs feel weak and shaky. I want to explain, but the words won't come. My eyes are hot, my throat tight. *It's over.*

"She dropped her phone," Paige says. Or is it Brooke? The sisters sound alike.

"Did she pass out?"

"Did you eat today?" Kayla asks urgently.

"Oatmeal," I manage to say over the lump of emotion lodged in my throat. Nausea threatens. I only managed to get two spoonfuls down with my nerves. I cross my arms, hugging myself tightly. More than two years together, most of that living together, and now poof! Gone. On our wedding day. A moan escapes. I can't manage speech.

I close my stinging eyes and curl on my side.

Kayla shifts to speak softly near my ear. "Sweetie, you're scaring me. Do we need to call an ambulance?"

I force myself to sit up. The last thing I want is doctors poking at me. "No, I don't need a doctor."

"We were knocking on the door and calling you, but you weren't answering," Kayla says. "We found something blue for you."

"Something blue," I echo.

"Something old, something new, something borrowed, something blue. I know it's super traditional, but I thought it was a nice touch."

Paige hands me my phone.

My hand is shaking, but I manage to pull up the text from Kevin and show her the screen.

"Shit!" Paige exclaims.

Brooke grabs the phone, and she and Kayla exclaim in outraged unison, "No!"

The sisters start talking over each other, and I collapse back on the bed, staring blankly at the ceiling.

"Someone has to stall the magazine people."

"This has never happened before."

"There was that one runaway bride—"

"*Never* happened."

"Do we have another couple we could find last minute to elope?"

"Gage and Skylar! They just got engaged, and they helped renovate and decorate the inn!"

"Great angle! I'm on it!"

The sisters race out the door. Hot tears leak out of my eyes. I've never been a crier. Nothing has ever hurt this much. My life has gone according to my careful plans...until now. I press a fist to my lips, the betrayal like a punch to the gut.

What happened? He never gave any indication that he was having second thoughts. There's no logic, no reason.

Kayla rushes back in a moment later. "I'm so sorry. Can I help you out of your gown? Give you a ride home? I can drive you as soon as I finish talking to…"

The sound of her voice trails off as I lose focus. Too many words to comprehend while emotion clogs every logical part of my brain. I bite my lower lip, my eyes hot. I was going to ride home with Kevin. Where did he go? Maybe he went to work at the lab, unfazed by the end of our relationship forever. He often works on Saturdays.

"What can I do for you?" Kayla asks urgently.

I close my eyes. "I just need to rest a bit here, okay?"

"Okay, you rest." She takes off my heels, pulls the blanket over me, and arranges the pillow under my head. "I'll be back."

The door closes behind her. After a few more minutes of leaking tears, my brain starts working again, trying to figure out where I went wrong with my calculations. I was so sure of Kevin. The odds were good. Better than good. An almost one hundred percent certainty of a successful union. Nothing is one hundred percent, but…

The first lick of anger has me throwing off the covers and swinging my legs off the bed, my feet firmly planted on the floor. A text? He dumps me on our wedding day *by text*? After two years and two months together of perfect compatibility!

Only it obviously wasn't perfect.

Up is down; left is right; right is wrong, wrong, wrong.

If I could be wrong about him, then my careful calculations no longer apply to *any* part of my life.

I stand, my legs a little shaky, and wipe tears from my cheeks. Now my grandparents won't meet my new husband on our honeymoon in Las Vegas. My grandparents retired there. They're the only family members who knew about the elopement, and they couldn't wait to meet Kevin once it was official.

Only now there won't be a honeymoon.

I move zombielike over to the window. Levi, the wedding officiant, stands in place by the wedding pergola. The sisters are scattered to the wind. Who knows where they went to salvage the situation, probably huddled with the magazine people. It's just Levi out there, completely ignorant of anything that's happened.

I should tell him the wedding's off.

I shove my feet into my sneakers, stuff my phone in my purse, and rush downstairs and outside. He straightens when he sees me barreling down the short aisle toward him, a bride with no groom.

"Is everything okay?" he asks.

I stop short in front of him, heart galloping with my race to get here and finish this whole damn wedding business, and then look up into warm brown eyes. I'm beyond jolting at this point, but they do something to me, offering a safe oasis in the storm of my life. Kevin's eyes are blue, an icy cold blue. He's always calm and collected. I found the lack of drama from him a sign of our harmonious relationship. Now I have to wonder if he ever really loved me at all. My lower lip wobbles, my eyes stinging.

"Galena, are you okay? What's going on?"

No, nothing is okay, and I'm not sure it ever will be again. I struggle to find the words to explain what's happened and the uncertainty of life as I know it, but what comes out is barely a whisper, "The wedding's off."

He puts an arm around my shoulders, guiding me to the white tent, where a few round tables with chairs are set out.

"Have a seat," he says, guiding me to a chair.

I sit, swallowing hard.

A moment later, he's crouching by my side, offering me a cold bottle of water from an ice bucket set on a nearby table. "Here, drink."

I take a long swallow, the cool liquid soothing the tightness of my throat. A breeze wafts through the tent, smelling of sweet summer flowers. It would've been a beautiful wedding. I bite my quivering lower lip.

"Do you want to talk about it?" he asks.

"No."

"Okay."

I drink more water, unsure where to go from here. At least I'm not shaking anymore. I set the bottle on the table.

"Do you need me to talk to Paige?" he asks.

I meet his concerned eyes and suddenly wish he could take me away from all this. I press my lips together and shake my head.

"What can I do for you?"

He really seems to care. "No wonder you're a popular mayor," I blurt. "You're willing to help when people need it the most."

He takes my hand, giving it a squeeze. It's both comforting and electrifying. "Where did everyone go?"

I look back at the wedding pergola, my heart lurching at the empty scene. "To find a new wedding couple, I guess."

"Galena—"

I turn back to him. "I need to get out of here. Now. With you."

He stands and offers his hand to help me up. I place my hand in his larger one, warmth enveloping my fingers, a tingle rushing up my arm.

"Have you ever ridden a motorcycle?" he asks.

I stare at him, my mouth forming an O of surprise. "I've never been on a motorcycle in my life because statistically speaking—" I stop myself. "Never mind. It sounds fun."

He smiles, crinkles forming at the corners of his eyes. Warmth spreads through me from head to toe. "Yeah?"

I nod once, trying to look like the kind of woman who enjoys riding off on motorcycles with men who give them jolts and calmness in equal measure. Whatever the reason, Levi puts me off-balance.

He takes my hand in his. "Okay, then. Let's go."

My legs feel like jelly as I follow him blindly through a side yard. Adrenaline? Pure terror? Excitement? I have no clue. This is my new life with zero calculations before doing a thing. I'm going by instinct.

The moment the wedding pergola is behind me, I relax. The hard part is over. I'm getting out of here.

We arrive at his Harley motorcycle, which he immediately straddles, starting the engine, and I don't hesitate, hitching up my wedding gown and climbing on. Wow, look at me. Spontaneous, impulsive, a risk-taker. The anti-Galena is in full force. Or is it Galena 2.0?

I wrap my arms around Levi's waist, and we're off. My stomach jumps, vibrations rocking through me, and I hang on a little tighter.

Moments later, I'm able to loosen my grip as we ride. The wind in my hair and the warm sun on my face soothes me. Everything in my life is completely out of control, yet at this moment I don't feel panicky at all. I rest my cheek against Levi's warm back. I feel safe.

~

Levi

So sue me, I hoped they would break up before the wedding. That sounds terrible, but there it is. I've never felt such an instant attraction to someone. The first time we met, Galena seemed like a woman comfortable in her own skin with her faded Wonder Woman T-shirt and jeans. Her large black-framed glasses magnified her chocolate brown eyes. And those eyes are sharp with intelligence. Her demeanor was confident and sure. I couldn't wait to get to know her better until I realized she wasn't at the inn with Kayla for a visit. She was there to plan her wedding. The groom wasn't with her then.

The more I ran into Galena around town, the more appealing she became. She's beautiful, smart, and a little quirky, an irresistible combination. Kevin was never with her. Then I started hearing bad stuff about him. Kayla and her husband, Adam, my next-door neighbors, went on a double date with them. Adam said never again because the guy was a selfish ass. Kayla thought so too and said that Galena's sister didn't like him either, which was part of the reason Galena planned to elope.

I dreaded officiating for them, but I'd already committed to doing it. I would never go back on my word, especially with the *Leisure Travel* people there to feature the inn. Now she's finally single. I try to tamp down my happiness in light of her current distress. Clearly, Kevin didn't deserve her. I need to wait for the right timing.

I head in the direction of Lake Summerdale since the view of the water surrounded by trees is relaxing for most people. I'm not sure what I'm dealing with here—a runaway bride or a jilted bride. All I know is she needed help.

Galena hugs me close, warming my back. How many times have I imagined getting closer to her, and now here she is.

I park in a secluded spot near a large weeping willow tree with low-hanging branches that brush the water. I look over my shoulder at Galena, who loosens her hold on me. Her hair is wild, tossed by the wind. She's the most beautiful bride I've ever seen. And I've seen a lot, being the wedding officiant at the Inn at Lovers' Lane. "Hi."

"Hi!" She looks a little dazed. "This is a nice spot. Soothing."

"Good. You get off the bike first."

She does, and I follow suit. She lifts her wedding gown so it doesn't trail on the ground as she heads to the shoreline. She's wearing white sneakers under her gown. I like that. She does things her own way. I bet she has an inner wild woman she sets free on the regular.

I join her as she looks at the view. "I wasn't sure where you wanted to go. I could take you out of town if you want." *I could take you all the way to California! I'm up for anything.*

Her eyes never leave the lake. "Here's fine. My house is a

block away, about a third of the way around the lake in that direction." She points over to it. "Sunset Lane. Ever notice how the lake is like a wheel hub with the streets jutting out like spokes?"

"Yeah, the town founders designed it that way so the lake was the center of the social scene and bike paths could connect everything. It was utopia for the hippie founders back in the sixties. I'm one street over from you on Harmony Lane, right next door to Kayla and Adam."

Her eyes well. "Oh, yeah? Lucky you. Maybe we should've bought a house on Harmony Lane instead. Then we'd have harmony instead of the sunset of our relationship." She wipes tears from her face furiously.

I stand quietly by her side, giving her time to regain her composure.

After a few minutes, she turns to me. "Sorry."

"Not at all. What happened back there? Did you change your mind?"

"No. He…oh, here, I'll show you." She pulls her phone from her purse and shows me the text.

I mutter a curse. "Coward move. He doesn't deserve you."

Her head whips toward mine. "You don't even know me that well."

"I know you're a good person, and no one deserves to be left on their wedding day by a stupid text."

"Yeah, well…"

"Want me to have him thrown in jail? I'm the mayor; I've got connections."

She smiles, but her eyes are still shiny with tears. "That would be really nice."

I fight the urge to pull her into my arms, soothing her tears away. Maybe we should get back on my Harley so she can hug me again. That way *she* can initiate contact.

She rubs a hand over her face. "I'm wiped out." Her breath hitches, and she blinks rapidly. "Gah! Can a person be sad and mad at the same time?"

"Absolutely. How about I take you home? You can get out of this wedding dress and into something more comfortable."

She nods but then stills. "Kevin might be there. I don't think I can deal with him right now. I might throw something at him."

"Kick him out. You deserve some peace."

"We co-own the house." She huffs. "Screw it. You're right. I deserve some peace." She taps her phone and then puts it to her ear. A few moments later, she tells me, "Voicemail."

She texts him instead.

As soon as she finishes, I ask, "Ready?"

She turns to go and then stops, staring at her phone. "Dammit. He says he's not moving out because the house is half his, and he'll be back tonight after work." A hard expression comes over her face, her chin jutting out. "I'm not moving out. This is the first time I've ever lived in a house instead of an apartment."

"Sounds complicated. Wait. He went to work after walking out on your wedding?"

"I don't want to talk about it," she mutters.

We walk back to my Harley.

"How did you like the ride?" I ask.

"I loved it. I avoided it before because the odds of injury compared to car travel—nope! I don't live my life by calculations anymore."

I get on the bike. "I'm not sure what you mean. Your life is a calculation?"

She hitches up her gown and climbs on behind me, hugging me tight. "Just drive or *ride*, if that's the right term. Ride!"

I smile, put on my helmet, and take off toward her house. I need to get a second helmet. There's wild and then there's basic safety. I haven't had a passenger before today. The Harley is a recent purchase when I decided to look beyond my long list of duties and responsibilities and let my inner wild man break free. Nothing says freedom like riding your Harley on the open road.

A few minutes later on Sunset Lane, she yells, "This one!"

I pull into the driveway of her house and park. It's a two-story colonial-style home, white with black shutters and a painted red door. Most of the homes in town are like this, built in the seventies, except for the original cottages around the lake from the sixties. Even those have started being replaced by larger modern homes.

She climbs down and smiles shyly at me, looking radiant despite how upset she was a short while ago. My heart kicks harder. "I feel surprisingly safe with you. I mean riding with you."

"I plan on buying a second helmet for passengers." *That means you're invited.*

"Smart. Do you have time to come in for a bit?"

I hide my surprise at the invitation. I didn't think a jilted bride would be up for company. "Absolutely." I get off my bike, telling myself I'm just going to make sure she's okay. Not the time to make a move.

I follow her inside her house. The place is extremely neat with minimal stuff. Just past the entryway, I get a glimpse of the living room to my right. There's a navy sofa and a glass coffee table with nothing on it.

"I'm going to change," she says and heads upstairs. "Have a seat anywhere."

I flop down on the sofa, which is more comfortable than it looks. A TV is mounted on the wall across from the sofa. Not sure where the remote is. The nearby dining room has a small round wooden table with four chairs. The walls are white, hardwood floors bare. Maybe they didn't have time to make it look more lived-in. Guess I had a head start on that since I bought the house I grew up in from Mom when she retired from teaching and moved to Savanna, Georgia. My sister is in Germany with her Air Force husband, so she didn't want the place. They move frequently.

I check my phone, which I turned off for the ceremony earlier. I always do that out of respect for the couple. Oh, shit. There's a lot of texts and voicemails from Paige. They want me back at the inn to marry Gage and Skylar for the *Leisure Travel* article. That was fast. They just got engaged last week. I bet they're just doing it to help out Paige, their former client.

Stomping overhead reminds me of Galena's predicament. I need to stay until she's okay. Where's her friend Kayla in all this? Probably helping her sisters set up a substitute wedding. Well, they can get a substitute wedding officiant. Skylar and Gage don't have enough time to get a wedding license, so it wouldn't be the real deal anyway. I seem to remember Skylar declaring the whole town would be invited to their wedding next summer at their lake house. They can go through the motions for the magazine people and still have the real wedding next summer like they planned. Galena is the priority here.

I send a quick text to Paige letting her know I'm with Galena and suggest Paige take my place. Then I set the phone to silent so I can focus on the jilted bride upstairs.

A few minutes later, Galena marches downstairs and strides toward me, clutching her balled-up wedding gown. She holds it out to me. "Here. You said you live next door to Kayla. Give this to her for someone else. She loves helping with weddings."

I stand and take the gown from her. Her hair's up in a messy bun, and she's wearing glasses again with the same faded Wonder Woman T-shirt she was in when I first met her and pink hearts pajama bottoms. I bet that T-shirt's her favorite. Or maybe her favorite clothes are packed for her honeymoon in her ex-fiancé's car. What a jerk. He left her stranded at the inn with no ride and went to work. "Anything else I can do for you?"

She runs a shaky hand through her hair, accidentally pulling locks of hair out of place in the process as she stares at the gown. "That's done."

"Why don't you have a seat, and I'll get you a drink."

Her eyes meet mine, and our gazes lock for an electric moment. She hugs me suddenly, the gown trapped between us.

"Thank you for the quick escape," she whispers.

I manage to pull a hand free from the gown and wrap an arm around her. "No problem."

She pats my back a few times and steps back. "I'm not usually much of a hugger. Hope that wasn't presumptuous."

I smile. "Once you ride together, hugging is part of the deal."

She smooths her hair back. "Right. Guess that's true. I hugged you all the way here, didn't I?"

"Yup. Hey, I don't mind sticking around when your ex returns, for moral support."

She takes a deep breath. "No, I need to face him myself. You'd better go now. I need to make a few phone calls."

"Okay, feel free to…"

She's already at the door, holding it open. I can take a hint. Guess I was just here to take the wedding gown out of her sight.

I shove the gown under one arm and pull my business card from my wallet, handing it to her. It's my mayor card with my personal phone number on it. For me, there's no separation of personal and professional. The Summerdale community is my second family. "That's my personal number on there. Call me if you need anything, even if it's just for a ride on my bike."

She looks at the card. "Thank you, Mayor Levi. Sorry you couldn't officiate a wedding today."

"It was for the best. Please just call me Levi."

"Okay, Levi. Bye."

"Bye." I look toward the door and then back at her. "You're awesome. Kevin didn't know what he had in you. I would."

Her eyes widen.

Too much?

I step out of the house and spy my black and chrome Harley, the symbol of my new take on life. Taking risks, open to new experiences. I swagger over to my bike and climb on. I did just fine back there. What's riskier than saying how you really feel to a woman you want?

On her jilted wedding day.

Crap. Timing is everything. I'll be lucky if she ever talks to me again.

3

—————

Galena

"I'll be okay." I give Kayla another hug. I have to. She keeps hugging me. We're standing by my front door in the longest goodbye of my life.

"Are you sure?" she asks, hanging onto my arms and looking deep into my eyes.

I nod. "I just need some alone time to decompress."

Kayla is the main reason I agreed to an elopement wedding at the inn. Her sisters needed an elopement couple they could count on because of the upcoming feature article on the inn and their elopement wedding packages. Who knew it would end the way it did? So much for logic and careful calculations. Life doesn't work that way, and it took today for me to learn that hard lesson.

Kayla searches my expression for signs of distress. I try to look less pathetic so she won't hug me again. I want to burrow under the covers in my soft bed. "Sorry I had to run out while you were still reeling from the news. We were all just so shocked and sprang into action to salvage the magazine shoot. I heard Levi brought you home. He's a good guy."

Even in my current state of shock and distress, a zing goes through me at his name. "He seemed that way, coming to my rescue the way he did."

"Yeah. He lives next door, so I see him all the time. Mostly because he's chasing his dog, Baxter, down. That dog's always making an escape. He has a mind of his own."

My limbs feel heavy. "Sounds like a difficult dog. I'm really tired."

She hugs me for the millionth time. "You rest. But please call me if you want me to come over with chocolate or you need backup when Kevin comes home." Kayla knows how to cover the essentials—company, chocolate, and support.

"I'm not worried about him. He'll probably act like nothing's happened. He's very unexcitable." *Kind of like a corpse.* Guess my dark side comes out after a disaster of a wedding day.

"Text me later tonight, okay?"

"Okay."

She leaves, and I shut the door behind her, leaning against it for a long moment. Visions of my earlier time at the inn preparing for the Big Day that turned out to be a big fat zero swim through my mind.

I drag myself upstairs to my bedroom. The moment I cross the threshold and see Kevin's stupid sheepskin slippers next to the bed and his latest fantasy novel on the nightstand, something in me snaps. I grab his pillow, the slippers, and his book, open the sliding glass door to the second-floor deck, and drop everything over the edge. It lands on the patio below. Great. If he wants to stick around, he can sleep on the patio. I don't even want him as close to me as the deck.

That felt so good that I go for the dresser drawers, emptying his clothes by the handful and dumping them over the edge too. I return to the bedroom and look around. Anything else? Ah. The bathroom. I go in there and empty his stuff from the medicine cabinet and the shower and hesitate. If I dump it, it might make a mess or even harm wandering wildlife. Wouldn't want a deer or raccoon chewing on a tube of toothpaste, would we? I toss it all in the trash except for his toothbrush and toothpaste. I have better plans for them. I swish his toothbrush around the toilet and put it back in the toothbrush holder. I'll keep my toothbrush separate in the medicine cabinet. Then I squeeze his toothpaste in the middle. He always rolls from the bottom in neat folds. Ha!

Galena 2.0 is awesome! Impulsive and spontaneous, getting her revenge.

God, I'm tired.

I walk to the bed and crash facedown for a much-needed nap.

When I wake, I go downstairs, help myself to a glass of water and call my older sister, Izzy, short for Isabella. "Hi, it's me."

"What's wrong?"

I'm about to spill my guts when she says, "Hold on." And then she whispers loudly, "Go watch your show in the chair across the room. I don't want you getting sick too. Amelia, baby, hang on. I'm coming with that cool washcloth."

"What's going on? Are the girls okay?"

"Amelia has a fever. I've got her set up on the couch in front of the TV. I'm trying to keep Grace out of her face so she doesn't get it too, but it's a losing battle. She wants to take care of her."

Aww. Grace is always taking care of her dollies too. She'll make a great doctor or nurse one day.

"I'll let you go," I say.

"Just hold on."

A couple of minutes later, she says, "Okay, everyone's settled. What happened?"

"I almost eloped today."

"What!"

I pull the phone away from my ear at her volume. When I put it back to my ear, she's on a roll. "...getting married without me! Without your family! What were you thinking?"

"I'm sorry. It made sense at the time, and now nothing makes sense. He texted me right before the ceremony. Here's his coward text." I copy and paste his text, sending it to her.

Dead silence.

"Izzy, did you get it?"

"Yeah, I got it. I knew there was a reason I didn't like him. I could never quite put my finger on it. Something about him said loser. And it was obvious he was selfish. Welp, he finally showed his true colors."

The tension in my shoulders eases. Izzy's always got my back. "It's too bad Amelia's sick. I could really use some Amelia and Grace cuddles today."

"Oh, honey. I'm sorry. You must feel awful. As soon as the girls are better, we'll get together. Promise."

A sharp cry bursts out. One of my nieces.

"Grace! What are you doing? You spilled juice all over her!" Then to me, "I gotta go. Love you. Hang in there."

I hang up and go straight to the freezer for my carton of rocky road ice cream. I open it up and gasp. Kevin ate nearly all of it! There's just a few drips at the bottom. He *knows* this is my ice cream. How dare he deplete my supply when I need it most! He could've at least replaced it. Bastard. Toilet toothbrush is too good for him.

My phone rings, and I check the caller. Grandmom. I was planning on calling her later to tell her the honeymoon is off. Just not yet. I let the call go to voicemail, feeling guilty. I grew up in a two-bedroom apartment in the Bronx with my parents, grandparents, and sister. Izzy and I shared a sofa bed in the living room. My family is tight. I can't believe I almost eloped without them. Fresh air. I need fresh air.

I step onto the back patio, look at the mountain of Kevin crap, and go right back in. That's why I eloped. I knew there was tension over Kevin. Izzy made it clear she didn't like him, and Mom told me not to move in with him. After we moved in, my parents pretended I lived alone.

Kevin was my first serious boyfriend, and everything seemed to mesh so well between us. It seemed like there was no risk whatsoever to moving in, especially since I spent most nights at his place anyway. It was convenient, and we both saved on rent. My parents didn't agree with my logical reasoning.

My mind drifts to Levi. The warmth of his smile, the jolt

that goes through me every time our eyes meet. That never happened with Kevin. We were more like roommates with nine a.m. scheduled Saturday sex. Maybe life with Kevin wasn't as great as I'd thought. Maybe the way I feel around Levi is what I should've been feeling for the man I was about to marry. Was I really about to sign up for a lifetime of dull scheduled sex?

My phone vibrates with a voicemail. I cringe but listen to it anyway.

Grandmom's voice comes through, strong and steady. "Hi, honey, just called to see how it went today and say—"

"Congratulations!" she and Grandpop say in unison.

"Can't wait to see you!" Grandpop says.

"Can't wait to meet your new husband!" Grandmom says. "See you soon! Bye!"

I was so looking forward to seeing them. It's been a year since I saw them last. No groom, no honeymoon in Las Vegas. I blink back tears and head upstairs. Enough of this wallowing. I'm going for a run to clear my head.

I change into a black tank top with a sports bra built in and switch my pajama pants for gray sweatpants. Lace up my sneakers, stretch, and I'm ready to go. I hear the front door open. My heart pounds as I make my way to the top of the stairs to finally face the coward who ditched me on our wedding day. In front of the magazine people too!

"Oh, you're here," Kevin says. He looks like he always looks when he comes home from work, quietly content. His short blond hair is mussed, jaw clean-shaven in preparation for today. He usually doesn't shave on the weekends. He's wearing his white dress shirt and dark gray suit pants like he went straight from our wedding to the lab. All he cares about is his research.

I walk downstairs and join him, where he's standing by the front door. "Get a lot done at work?"

"Yup. There's always more to do. We're on the final phase of—"

"Don't pretend like nothing happened today."

"It just didn't feel like the right time. I hope you're not mad."

"Mad? Of course I'm mad. I bought a gown. I got worked up over what was supposed to be the happiest day of my life, and you dumped me by text!"

"I didn't dump you. I just said I couldn't marry you." He gives me a patient smile. "I'd like to go back to the way it was before. Things were great between us, just living together."

"Well, Kevin, you can't go back in time and undo what's been done. We're over, and I don't think you should live here anymore."

He crosses his arms. "It's my house too. I'm not going anywhere."

My chest tightens, and I feel like I can barely get a breath. I'm not up to fighting this fight today. I need to regroup and find a way to get him out. "You can sleep in the guest room for tonight while you look for a new place. You're not welcome anywhere near me."

"Once you calm down and think this through rationally…"

I don't hear the rest because I'm out the door, heading toward the lake, needing to get far away from him.

Levi

I walk into my house, set the wedding gown over the back of the sofa, and head straight to the backyard for my dog, Baxter. He's a two-year-old beagle and an escape artist. I only planned to be out for an hour, so I let him stay on the back deck, where he likes to lounge under the patio table. The backyard is surrounded by a six-foot-tall wooden privacy fence with chicken wire along the bottom to prevent him from tunneling under it. It's as safe as I can possibly make it.

He's not here. Dammit. If I left him inside, he'd have gotten into my hamper again and chewed a hole in my shirt. I don't know how he always manages to find my most expensive shirts to destroy.

"Baxter!" I walk down the deck stairs into the yard and check under the deck. Nope. I survey the yard and spot a new hole. He started beyond the chicken wire and worked under it. I turn on my heel and go back to the house. Nothing keeps this dog contained. I started with a chain-link fence that he scaled and jumped off the top into the neighbor's yard, then I tried the invisible electric fence for dogs, and he ran right through it, and now I have an expensive high privacy fence, which he's managed to beat by tunneling under it.

I snatch his gray stuffed bunny, Walter, from the dining room floor, walk out the front door, and let myself through the gate into Adam and Kayla's backyard, hoping Baxter's there. Baxter reliably hunts Walter. Beagles were bred to hunt rabbits.

I give Walter a shake so he looks alive, the long ears and floppy arms and legs wiggling. "Baxter, look what I found! Walter escaped!"

No Baxter. I round the corner of the house and scan the yard, even checking in the tall plants of the garden.

A thud against glass gets my attention. Baxter is standing inside Adam's house, paws up on the glass patio door, white-tipped tail wagging. Looks like he decided to visit his friends, Adam's English bulldog, Tank, and light brown tabby cat, Simba. The trio look and act so different. Baxter looks thrilled to see me, Tank looks bored, and Simba is giving herself a bath.

I shake my head and make my way to the front door, ringing the bell. A chorus of barks goes up. A few minutes later, Adam appears at the front door. He's a master carpenter, tall and wiry with muscle. We go fishing on the lake together.

He jerks his chin at me. "Hey, I found Baxter in our backyard, so I let him in."

"Thanks. I'll take him home now."

"I think he wants a friend. He comes over to see Tank and Simba all the time."

"Sorry about that." I grab Baxter by the collar just as he attempts an escape out the front door. Tank just stands inside, staring at Baxter with his big serious bulldog eyes and squashed-in face. Simba peeks from around the corner of the dining room wall. "I've got my hands full with this one. I can't imagine another one like him." I scoop Baxter up, and he lunges for Walter the bunny in my other hand. I nearly drop both of them.

Adam reaches out to help, but I manage to hang onto beagle and bunny. "A pal might keep Baxter fully occupied."

"Maybe. Let me drop him off at home, and then I'll be back with a wedding gown for Kayla. Galena was just left at the altar and hoped Kayla could use it for another bride."

"Seriously? That sucks. Yeah, bring it by. I'm sure Kayla will find something to do with it. Poor Galena, though I didn't like Kevin. He barely paid attention to her when we all went out. Everything was about him."

"It was for the best." I head out, secretly pleased. She's better off, even though it's painful right now.

I bring Baxter back to my house and toss Walter to him, but Baxter's already moved on from stuffed-bunny hunting to sniffing for crumbs on the kitchen floor. He's got a world-class sniffer, and his long floppy ears help bring more scents toward him. He's mostly white fur with large black areas and reddish brown markings on his head, ears, and back. He's a purebred. Hard to believe he was left at the shelter when he was a year old. Apparently, it happens a lot with beagles because the owners or neighbors can't deal with the volume of beagle sounds. They bark, bay (sounds like a dog yodel), and howl. Not great for apartment living with close neighbors, but just fine out here in the suburbs. Besides, it's just me at home, and I don't mind his sounds.

After I give Galena's gown to Adam, I come home and change out of my suit. What a day. I only started officiating wedding ceremonies a year ago when the Inn on Lovers' Lane opened. The owners asked me if I would, and I learned that mayors can legally perform the deed. It's a side gig, easy money for a short amount of time. It hasn't become routine either. It's actually really cool to watch the ceremony play out with each couple, seeing the love between them expressed in different ways. People fascinate me.

I feed Baxter and heat up some leftover Chinese takeout for myself. There's only enough pork lo mein for a snack. I should pick up a real dinner from The Horseman Inn after I take Baxter on his walk. I eat over the sink, looking out the window at the backyard. What would keep Baxter in? I'm starting to think I need to build a dome with skylights. A beagle biosphere. Ha.

A few minutes later, he's finished his dinner, so I let him out back, keeping an eye on him. He does his business and runs right back. He knows the routine. We usually go for an after-dinner walk around the lake if it's still light out.

I finish my dinner, toss the take-out container, and grab his leash from the hook by the back door. "Time for a walk."

He jumps excitedly, understanding "walk." I crouch down and give him some love, petting him behind his ears the way he likes before I snap on his leash. "I know you long for wild adventures, but you have to stop escaping on me. One day I might not find you."

He looks up at me with his big brown velvety eyes, looking innocent.

My heart softens, but I keep my voice firm. "I mean it, or you're going to have to be locked inside all the time. Unless I'm right there to watch you in the yard. Is that what you want?"

He licks my face.

I stand, wiping my cheek. He races to the front door, the leash flying out behind him. Time for our next adventure. I should get a sidecar for my Harley. Then Baxter and I could escape together.

When we get to the end of the block, I see a dark-haired woman sprinting across Lakeshore Drive, heading toward the path around the lake. Is that Galena? Baxter jerks the leash from my hand as he races toward her. Shit! What if a car comes?

I run as hard as I can and catch up to Baxter at the side of the road, where he's suddenly become interested in sniffing a Stop sign. I grab his leash and give him a stern lecture on running off.

"Do you always talk to your dog like he understands English?" a feminine voice asks.

My lips curve up. Baxter brought me to the woman I can't stop thinking about. Good boy.

4

———

I was nearly across Lakeshore Drive when I felt a pebble in my sneaker and had to stop. That's when I heard a man giving a stern lecture to a floppy-eared dog sniffing a Stop sign pole. Levi. *The good guy.* Kayla said so, and he's been good to me so far.

Levi grins, closing the distance between us, dog in tow. Warmth floods me. A lot of warmth. Heat really. I've never had such a visceral reaction to a guy.

Not that I have a lot of experience. Kevin was the first guy I ever got serious about. In fact, he was my first. Yes, I was a twenty-four-year-old virgin. I wasn't raised in a sex-positive environment to say the least, and honestly, no guy ever appealed enough to make me want to go there. Kevin is almost exactly like me—practical and analytical—so I felt comfortable right away. I'm beginning to think comfort is overrated.

Levi's brown eyes sparkle with good humor. "I don't speak beagle, so English is the best I can do."

I smile and crouch down to pet his dog. He looks up at me with his big brown eyes and gets close, sniffing my ear. I laugh.

"This is Baxter, expert escape artist. He got away from me

running to you. I think when he saw you running, he thought it was a game of chase."

"You can chase me anytime," I tell Baxter as he licks my neck, making me giggle. I straighten and look into Levi's eyes as he searches my expression. He's wondering how the jilted bride is doing.

I look out to the lake, a soft breeze causing a ripple across the water, the green leaves of the surrounding trees swaying gently. The breeze feels good on my skin. I keep my focus on the present moment. No use in rehashing the jilted-bride situation from earlier today.

"How're you holding up?" Levi finally asks, gesturing for me to join them on their walk. He's dressed casually now in a blue T-shirt and khaki shorts, and something about him makes me relax, like I can trust him.

"I went through shock and anger, so I guess now I'm on my way to acceptance."

"That was fast. Good for you."

"Well, my ex, Kevin, helped that along. He came home and acted like nothing happened. He actually thought we could go back to status quo."

"Wow. He sounds clueless."

"That about sums it up. So I told him to look for a new place. For now I guess he's in the guest room. Or the patio. That's where I threw all his clothes."

"Do you feel safe at home?"

I glance at him, touched he cares. It's not like we know each other that well. "He's harmless. All he cares about is his research. He's working on the genomic—you don't care about that. *I* don't care about that anymore. And it's not like we had an off-the-wall sex life." I slap a hand over my mouth. This is not my sister or Kayla. I'm just frazzled enough from today's events not to have my usual reserve.

He laughs. "It's fine. People tell me all kinds of stuff as mayor. They want me to fix their problems."

"Sorry. You're just so, I don't know, accepting. I feel like I could tell you anything, and you'd just say, okay, what do you want to do next?"

He smiles, the corners of his eyes crinkling. My chest warms at that smile. "I'm glad you feel that way. So your ex is more interested in science than you, did I get that right?"

"We're both busy professionals, and honestly, I didn't mind the sex-on-Saturday-morning schedule since I had time to…" I stop myself, laughing a little at my oversharing. "Let's just say it probably wouldn't be all that different for him to move into the guest room."

"Sounds like a tame relationship. Not so much passion like you might hope for in someone you're going to spend the rest of your life with."

Exactly what I've been thinking. "I looked at it from every angle, calculated the odds of success, and I was—" I sigh "—dead wrong."

"It happens."

What an understanding guy.

I find myself sharing more. "That's why I've decided to be Galena 2.0, a spontaneous risk-taker."

"I decided that recently too. Take some risks, have an adventure. We could have some fun with that."

I give him a sideways glance. *Is he flirting with me?* I don't typically inspire that in men. My sister says I hide behind my large black-framed glasses and old broken-in clothes. My T-shirts and jeans are super soft with age—perfection—but I don't consider that hiding. I'm just being myself. I do dress appropriately for work, mostly in blouses and tailored pants with flats.

Welp, the moment of possible flirting passed, and it's not like I know how to flirt back anyway. Would I even want to start something on my disaster of a wedding day? So what if Levi's handsome and kind and just edgy enough to inspire thoughts of riding off with him on his Harley to destinations unknown. I need a friend more than another man in my life.

We stop by the shade of a tall sugar maple tree that Baxter seems especially interested in sniffing.

I take a deep breath of fresh air. A family of ducks swims by—a mama followed by four fluffy baby ducks. So cute! Over to my right, there's a couple in a rowboat, and farther down the path, kids riding bikes. Why haven't I taken the time to visit the lake? I live a block away, and all I did was view it through my telescope from the second-story deck. I'm done with tame, distant relationships. From now on, I'm going to be up close and personal with the lake. And with people too.

Baxter's nose presses against the back of my knee, surprising me. I turn and pet him. Dogs too, buddy. Up close and personal.

Levi skips a stone across the lake. "Beautiful, isn't it? I've lived here my whole life, and I never get tired of looking at it. Every season is spectacular, especially the fall."

I take in the lake view, trying to commit it to memory. It's so peaceful here. "I'm looking forward to seeing it then."

He's quiet, and I sense he's looking at me. A sudden bout of nerves has me filling the silence. "I'm glad you were there for me today back at the inn and after and now too. I didn't plan this part or the other."

"I'm glad too. The first time we met, I thought you were someone I wanted to get to know better."

I meet his eyes, and my entire body heats, my pulse fluttering erratically. He's definitely flirting, and he's very direct. "Do you always speak so freely?"

"It's something new I'm trying out when I meet a woman I really like."

I tuck a loose lock of hair behind my ear, suddenly hyper-aware of myself. I'm wearing my running clothes with my hair thrown into a messy bun. No contacts either. I'm wearing the glasses my sister says hide my beauty. Maybe Levi sees an inner beauty that most men miss. "Thank you." My voice sounds hoarse. "I like you too."

"How about we grab a bite at The Horseman Inn? It's a short walk from here."

I think about what dinner will be like at my house, most

likely with Kevin eating nearby while reading some scientific journal on his phone, and promptly agree. "Sounds good. I've been there a couple of times and liked it."

"Great. I'll just need to get Baxter settled at home. Do you want to meet there in half an hour, or I could stop by your place, and we could walk over together."

Kevin probably wouldn't like to see another guy at the house to take me to dinner. It would seem like a date on the very day we broke up. Is it a date?

"I'll meet you there," I say.

"Ready to head home now, or did you want to finish your run?"

"I'm hungry. Let's go now."

He turns to Baxter. "Let's go. Come on, boy."

Baxter slowly gets up from the shade of the tree where he was napping and stretches his front and back legs. Then he looks up at Levi expectantly. Levi gives him a pet and starts walking.

I join them. I kinda want to ask if he thinks this is a date, but then again I don't want to make things awkward. There's only so much emotional turmoil a jilted bride can take in a day.

He gives me a charming lopsided smile. "What did you think of me when we first met?"

My cheeks warm, remembering how I was instantly drawn to him, and it puzzled me because I was at the inn to plan my elopement wedding. I shouldn't have given him a second look, yet I couldn't take my eyes off him. I can't say any of that. "Uh, well, Kayla told me you were the mayor, and I thought it was unusual to be so young and already on your second term. Also, you seemed really relaxed and comfortable talking about a wedding with a group of women."

"I can talk to anyone. You have to understand I grew up here. The Summerdale community is like family to me."

Baxter lunges forward, barking at an approaching black miniature poodle, who stares at him, showing no fear. Levi tightens the leash, and the woman holding the poodle tightens her leash.

"Hi, Terri, how're the kids?" Levi asks as we get close.

Baxter goes to sniff the butt of the poodle, who yips and turns quickly away.

"They're good, thanks. How're you?"

"Can't complain. Terri, this is Galena…" He turns to me. "Sorry, I forgot your last name."

"Torres. Galena Torres." I shake her hand. "I just moved here a couple of months ago."

"Welcome! You picked a good person to show you around."

I smile. "I've seen the lake twice today, which is more than the entire time I've lived here, except for a distant view from my deck."

"Oh, are you lucky enough to live on Lakeshore Drive?" Terri asks.

I consider saying I view the lake a block away through my telescope, but quickly decide that sounds too nerdy. Sometimes you just want to play it cool. Like when you're with the sexy mayor of Summerdale.

I gesture toward my street. "I live a block away. I can see it from my second-story deck."

She cocks her head. "Yeah?"

"Mmm-hmm." No superpowered telescope viewing here. Just superpowered vision. This is why people think I'm odd, except for Kayla and my sister. They understand me.

Levi smiles at Terri. "We're heading over to The Horseman Inn for dinner. Nice to see you."

"Enjoy your date!" she says and moves on, her poodle hurrying to keep up.

"We're just friends!" I call after her. I feel compelled to explain we're not on a date since Kayla told me gossip spreads fast in town.

She turns back and looks to Levi and then back to me with a big smile. "Okay. Bye."

Baxter pulls to follow the poodle, but Levi commands in a

deep baritone, "Come." A hot shiver runs down my spine. Baxter follows Levi immediately. Dear Lord, I'd follow that deep commanding voice too. I'm tingling in places I have no business tingling in.

I sneak a look at Levi as we walk. His beard is *hot*. "You must know everyone."

"Pretty much. I'll introduce you around."

"I already know Kayla and her sisters."

"I've never seen you out with them."

"I haven't been around much between work and going to my sister's place. She's a single mom, so I spend a lot of time at her apartment, hanging out with her and the girls. Or babysitting so she can get a break to do life stuff." My sister's husband cheated on her, and she's a no-second-chances kind of woman. My parents thought they should've tried to work it out for the sake of the children. In their view, marriage is forever.

"You like kids?" Levi asks.

"My nieces are the world to me."

"Interesting."

"What?"

"I seem to remember you mentioning your ex didn't want kids, so you wouldn't be taking his name."

I explained that to Kayla in front of everyone at the inn during the elopement planning meeting. I didn't think Levi was paying that close attention to me.

I glance at him. "Wow, you remember a lot from the first time we met."

"You made an impression."

Every nerve ending springs to life, making me feel hyper awake. I made an impression on him without even trying. This is so far from my normal with guys, I blurt, "I don't know why."

"Just a fact. So your nieces are your world, yet you weren't planning to have kids."

"Well, that's back on the table now, isn't it? I didn't want to have kids with someone who didn't want them."

"Fair enough. Tell me about your nieces."

So I do. I can talk about Amelia and Grace all day. They're so funny and cute and smart.

Next thing I know, we're back at my place.

"Sorry I talked your ear off," I say.

"I loved hearing it. See you at The Horseman Inn in half an hour, or if you need more time—"

"I'll be there in twenty. I'm starving. Kevin ate my rocky road ice cream, and I was too nervous to eat much before the wedding."

"Then we're definitely getting you ice cream after. Have you been to Summerdale Sweets?"

"Not yet. Kayla says it's divine."

He smiles his crinkly-eyed smile that I'm growing to love. It's so genuine and warm. "See you in a bit."

"Bye," I say in a breathy voice.

I rush inside my house, shocked by the sound of my own voice. Galena 2.0 comes with all sorts of surprises.

Kevin's on the sofa in the living room with his laptop, eating a granola bar. "You didn't go to the grocery store today?"

I clench my jaw. "No, Kevin. I was too busy going to a nonexistent wedding and then leaving on a nonexistent honeymoon." I hurry upstairs to change out of my running clothes.

"I'll order something," he calls. "Want anything?"

"There's no delivery here!" I call back. Kevin doesn't like to go out after work.

"Crap. When are you going to go to the store?"

"Never!" I yell, locking the bedroom door behind me to change. I swear we're going to get a few things straight tomorrow. We're *not* in a relationship anymore, and I don't have to do anything for him. The big whiny baby. I was very caring and domestic with him, taking care of the food shopping and cooking. I even packed his lunch for him every day. No more!

I change into a light blue T-shirt that's so old it's buttery soft. Only soothing things for me today. I eye my comfortable jeans with frayed knees. Is that good for a first date? I shake my head at myself. This isn't a date. Levi's just a nice guy who invited me to dinner. Two people can have a friendly dinner without it meaning anything romantic.

I pull on my newer jeans without holes and loose threads. They're stiffer, but more presentable for dinner with the mayor. He knows everyone and will likely introduce me to more people tonight. I brush out my hair and clean my glasses. There. Ready to go. I don't mind being early. The less time I spend at home, the better.

I head downstairs. "I'm going out."

"Are you going to the grocery store? Get the whole milk this time."

I work hard to stay civil. "You'll have to buy your own groceries from now on. I'm going to dinner with a friend."

"Geez, Galena, it's not like you don't have to eat too."

I exhale sharply. "Kevin, it's over. You get that, right? You're on your own for food and anything else you need from now on. I want you to find a new place as soon as possible. Tomorrow we'll figure out a plan. You'll excuse me if I'm not up to discussing all the particulars on the day you left me at the altar."

I head out the door.

"I texted you before you got to the altar!" he yells after me.

I throw up my middle finger and keep walking. It's really not like me to make obscene gestures, but this is Galena 2.0. How could I ever have thought Kevin was my dream guy? Just because we never fought? Was I really going to spend the rest of my life with a man so emotionally stunted he doesn't understand that walking out on our wedding means the end of our relationship?

I walk briskly down the street, eager to put more distance between us, and looking forward to spending more time with a *good* guy. The wild kind who rides a Harley. Maybe that was my type all along, and it took the rise of Galena 2.0 for me to realize it.

I may read too many superhero comics.

It hits me that I could be the superheroine in my own life, and that puts a bounce in my step. I like it.

5

———

Levi

I show up early for our dinner, and she's already here. Did she look forward to this as much as I did, or is she just one of those people who's always early? Doesn't matter. She's here, looking sexy with her dark hair down, wearing a clingy T-shirt and jeans that show off her hourglass figure. There's something so cute about her glasses too. They make her look like a brainy scientist just waiting to let loose.

She waves to me. "Hi, I got here a little early. Things are tense at home."

My joy at seeing her deflates with the reminder she's living with her ex. What if she tries to work things out with him?

What if she's in danger?

I close the distance. "What happened?"

She exhales sharply. "He wanted me to go grocery shopping for him. He's convinced we can go right back to being a couple who lives together." She shakes her head. "I took care of all that stuff for him before."

"You want me to talk to him?"

She studies me for a moment, her brows knit together. "No, that's okay."

"If you need a place to crash, I've got lots of room." Her

eyes widen, and I realize I've overstepped. "Or Kayla's place next door. She'd probably love to have you too."

She inclines her head. "I can always head to my sister's place if I need a break. Thanks anyway."

I go up to the host station. "Table for two. Could we have the corner table in the front dining room?"

The young guy hosting grabs two menus. "Right this way."

The front dining room has a large stone fireplace and several square dark wood tables for two or four people. There's a back dining room added on in the seventies and, across from it, the bar, where locals gather to watch the game on the TVs behind the bar or just hang out.

We follow the host to our table, a quiet intimate spot. The host holds out Galena's chair for her, and she says, "Oh! Thank you!" Seems like she's not used to gentlemanly manners. Another strike against her ex. I would've done it if the host weren't so quick.

I take the seat across from her.

She looks around. "I've only sat in the bar area before. This is nice with the huge fireplace."

"It's the original fireplace from the eighteenth century. This used to be a stagecoach stop between New York City and Boston."

"Cool."

We look over the menus. A waiter appears the moment we set the menus down, and takes our order. Galena orders the Kobe burger, truffle fries, and a chocolate shake. I'm glad she's not the kind of woman who just picks at a salad. I order chicken parmigiano, one of my favorites on the menu.

After the waiter leaves, I search Galena's expression for signs of distress after getting dumped at her wedding today. She seems okay, so I don't remind her of it. "So what parts of Summerdale have you checked out so far? I could give you a highlights tour. We'll be done in an hour."

She laughs. "I haven't seen too much, actually."

"Well, it's about time!" an older woman exclaims from just over my shoulder.

I let out a breath as Mrs. Joan Ellis approaches our table. She just turned ninety, white-haired but sharp as ever. She used to be my third-grade teacher, a strict no-nonsense woman who's known by all—secretly—as General Joan for her stern nature. She has no filter and says whatever's on her mind. Lately, that's been finding love for the single people in town. She imagines herself as Cupid. If only she knew we all see her as a general!

I force a pleasant expression, even though I'm inwardly cringing. The woman has made it her mission to see me married off to someone, anyone. It's embarrassing the way she sings my praises in front of unsuspecting women. And she's always asking me if I'm getting enough to eat in my lonely bachelor house. I'm not lonely. I've got Baxter. And it's not like I never have dates. People in town are always introducing me to their daughters, nieces, cousins, and granddaughters. One of the perks of working and living in the town I grew up in is that I rarely have to make an effort to meet someone. Women are constantly thrown in my path. Like the whole town wants to see their mayor married off. Not that anyone has really clicked for me, but I'm *not* lonely.

"Hi, Mrs. Ellis, how are you?" I ask.

"Just fine, thanks. Good to see you out for a decent meal instead of reheated takeout in your lonely bachelor house." She turns her sharp gaze to Galena. "Isn't he a fine young man?"

Heat creeps up my neck. See?

Galena's cheeks pinken. "Yes, but this isn't—"

"It's dinner," I say.

General Joan waves that away. "Your generation never wants to put a label on things. Doesn't change facts. Nothing wrong with courtship, especially with our mayor. Introduce us, Levi."

I jump in with the introductions. "Galena, this is Mrs. Joan Ellis. Mrs. Ellis, this is Galena Torres."

General Joan cocks her head. "Torres, interesting. Italian or Spanish? My husband's family had some Torres in there, Spanish background."

I didn't know that.

Galena fiddles with her cloth napkin. "Torres is Italian from my father's side. My mother's family is originally from Spain, then Argentina. She moved here for college and stayed when she met my dad."

I'd never ask someone's background so bluntly. Still, it's cool to hear. Galena's olive skin glows with good health. I wonder if her coloring is from the Italian or Spanish side. Probably both.

"Oh boy, Levi's got it bad," General Joan announces.

A few couples at nearby tables laugh.

"We're just friends," Galena insists.

"Yes." I send a dark look to the couples for laughing. I don't worry about winning votes among the townspeople. I always run unopposed. Either no one else wants the responsibility, or they're all content to keep me in office. The previous mayor was in office until he died at eighty-seven. It seems the mayor of Summerdale job is a life sentence. My chest tightens at the thought.

Is there another job I'd like to do? Am I making the most of my time here on earth? Is it meaningful? Significant enough? I've been asking myself the tough questions lately due to my dad's premature death at thirty-four. Am I passionate about being mayor, or duty-bound to give back to the community who got me through the most difficult time of my life?

General Joan pats my arm, interrupting my existential crisis. "Having it bad for a woman is good. Get with the lingo, Levi." She turns to Galena. "Do you like the beard? I fear it's verging on wild-man territory."

Galena's hand flutters in the air. "Uh, the beard is nice. Not too wild."

"Levi is good people," the General says with a decisive

nod. "You can't find a more responsible man. Now don't look at me like that, Levi. Responsible is the new sexy."

I choke on a laugh even as the heat in my neck creeps up to my face. "Are you here alone?"

She ignores my question in favor of torturing me further. "Hopefully you won't be eating alone in your lonely bachelor house much longer. Where did you two meet?"

I glance at Galena, who looks pained, and turn back to our heckler. "Who are you with tonight, Mrs. Ellis?"

"Harper and Caroline." Harper is her granddaughter, whom she raised. She was in my grade at school. Now she's a famous actor. Caroline is Harper's daughter. I'm guessing she's about two years old. I haven't seen either of them in a while.

The General continues in a conspiratorial tone to Galena, "Levi here took my Harper to the eighth-grade dance and did a fine job of following every rule I laid out for him." She turns to me. "I would've picked you for Harper if she hadn't run off to Hollywood."

Yes, the sexy rule follower. Thanks, Mrs. Ellis.

Galena tilts her head, looking thoughtful. Probably wondering who Harper is, since Mrs. Ellis mentioned Hollywood. Before I can mention where she might've seen Harper, the General says, "Harper's in the ladies' room, coaxing Caroline to use the potty. I told her to do what I did when Harper was little. Tell her she can wear the pretty panties if she uses the potty. Harper was potty-trained in two days."

I stifle a laugh. At least I'm not the only one she shares embarrassing details about.

Galena pipes up, "My nieces were trained in a week using M&M's and a reward chart."

"Hope they didn't rot their teeth," the General says.

"No, I don't think—"

"There's Harper now!" General Joan exclaims. "Well, was it a success?"

"Yes!" Harper says triumphantly as she walks toward us, holding a toddler on her hip. Caroline's light brown hair is in pigtails that curl. Harper has brown curls too. Her fierce-looking bodyguard, Joe, hovers in the background. He's got a shaved head, neck tattoo, and bulging muscles. Harper didn't used to have a bodyguard in town, but now that she has Caroline, he's always with her.

I smile at them and jerk my chin at Joe. He jerks his chin back and resumes his vigilant look around the place.

Harper beams at her daughter. "She's a pro now that she heard about the pretty panties with pink flowers."

General Joan cracks a rare smile. "See? Her grandmother's methods aren't outdated after all!"

"Great-grandmother," Harper says, kissing her cheek. Caroline reaches for her great-grandmother, and Harper hands her over.

"I am great," the General says, looking nearly soft as she talks to Caroline. "What a big girl you are!"

Caroline ducks her head shyly against her great-grand-mother's shoulder. A few people at nearby tables whisper about Harper. She grew up here, but there are still newcomers surprised to see a celebrity in person.

Harper turns and waves at them and then stops for a quick selfie with an excited group of ladies. She comes back to our table a moment later and smiles brightly at me. "Hi, Levi, how're you?"

"Good. It's been a while. This is—"

"Oh my God, you're Harper Ellis!" Galena exclaims. "I loved you in *Capital Asset* and *Living Gold* and *Dark Blade*. You were such a badass in *Dark Blade*. It was amazing and true to the original comic. Wow. I didn't know you lived here. I just moved here."

Harper smiles. "Nice to meet you…"

"Galena," she says, staring at Harper with an expression of awe.

"Welcome to Summerdale," Harper says. "I'm just visiting Grandmom while my husband is filming in Vancouver. He's part of the *Journey to the Galaxy* franchise. It's going to be epic."

"Garrett Rourke," I say to Galena, filling her in on Harper's husband.

Galena nods enthusiastically. "I know him. Well, I don't *know* him, like, in person, but wow." She puts a hand to her cheek, clearly overwhelmed.

Caroline reaches for Harper, and General Joan hands her over. "Mommy, when's Daddy coming home?" Wow, that was clear speech for such a little one.

Harper kisses her daughter's round cheek. "He's coming for a visit next weekend. That's just seven sleeps, and then we'll go visit him next time."

Caroline whispers in her mom's ear.

General Joan tells us, "I'm trying to convince Harper to film her next project on location here with her friend Claire Jordan's production company." Galena gasps at that famous actor's name, which the General ignores, probably used to all the fuss over famous actors. "They're based nearby in Connecticut. Harper's done some acting and directing for them. Claire likes to hire women directors because so few are given the chance to direct. Still behind the times in their industry."

"Filming here is a great idea," I say, thinking of the cast and crew that would bring to town, who'll want to explore a bit and spend some money. It could be good business for the inn, the grocery store, Summerdale Sweets, and The Horseman Inn. "We already have Sloane Robinson's TV show for the Turbo channel filming here at Murray's garage. You know *The Right Fix*?"

Harper laughs. "I'm the one who approached Sloane about the show. It helps that the garage is owned by her dad, so he can make it easy for scheduling."

"We'll find places for future projects," I say. "Just let me know what kind of locations you need, and I'll make it work."

"Thanks, Levi, you're the best." Harper gives my shoulder a squeeze. "I'm always happy for a chance to visit

Summerdale. Maybe we could put Grandmom in a movie too."

The General actually blushes, waving that away. "Nonsense. I don't want to be on camera."

Galena's eyes never leave Harper as she listens in rapt attention.

"You want a picture with Harper?" I ask Galena. "If it's okay with you, Harper."

"Sure," Harper says, putting Caroline down. "Just keep Caroline out of the frame. We're keeping her out of the spotlight."

Harper walks over to Galena's chair, and Galena pops up, handing me her phone with a shaking hand.

I want to tell her to chill. Harper's a sweetheart. I take their picture and hand back her phone.

"I want Daddy!" Caroline exclaims, looking beseechingly up at her mom. "Tell Daddy I'm a big girl now. When's Daddy coming home?"

Harper scoops her up. "Seven sleeps."

"Your daddy's working," General Joan says sternly.

"Daddy read story," Caroline says.

Harper turns to us. "We'd better go. It's near her bedtime, and she misses her daddy most then. The time difference makes it tough. Seems he's better at telling bedtime stories, if you can believe that."

Galena shakes her head solemnly. "She doesn't know what a great actor you are yet."

"Aww, thank you." Harper nudges my shoulder. "She's a keeper."

The three of them say a quick bye and hustle Caroline out the door as she gets louder and louder, asking for her daddy.

After they leave, Galena leans across the table toward me. "That was so exciting! I had no idea Harper was a local, and you took her to the eighth-grade dance too! What was that like?"

I lift one shoulder up and down. "She wasn't famous then,

so it was just like a regular eighth-grade date at the school gym. My mom drove us. I gave Harper a wrist corsage and had her home by nine thirty. That was a half hour before the dance ended, by the way. One of her grandmother's many rules before she agreed to let Harper go. Mrs. Ellis stopped by my house the day before the dance to thoroughly brief me on the rules for taking out her granddaughter, and then reviewed the rules the next day in front of Harper when I went to pick her up." I smile, shaking my head because it sounds funny in retrospect. Galena doesn't smile, just listens in rapt attention.

"What else?" she asks.

I think back to all the rules the General laid down. Something in there should make Galena laugh. It was way over the top. "While we were slow dancing, I had to leave enough room for Mrs. Ellis to walk between us, even though she wasn't there. She told me she had spies among the parent chaperones who'd be reporting back, and I believed her. I also had to refrain from unnecessary touching, never use a curse word, no sneaking out of the gym with her, and I had to tell Harper she was smart instead of pretty so Harper would never depend on her looks."

"I like that."

"It sort of backfired. Once we got to the dance, Harper asked me how she looked, and I told her she looked smart."

"So cool."

"I'm not sure Harper thought so." *Probably explains why we never had a second date.*

Galena tucks her hair behind her ears. "Was I too awkward fangirling over her?"

Yes. "No, not at all. I'm sure lots of people want a picture with *the* Harper Ellis."

"She kept her name for professional reasons just like I planned to do."

"Uh-huh."

"Normally I would keep quiet and just think how cool it was to meet her, but I'm being the new Galena, risk-taker, following my impulses, holding nothing back."

"Sounds like a great way to live. Why hold back? Go for what you want."

"Exactly! You were great with her grandmother too. She kept embarrassing you, and you never faltered."

"Yeah, well," I mumble, even more embarrassed that she noticed I was embarrassed. I'd hoped my beard covered any blush in my face.

"I'd love to introduce you to my grandparents."

"Yeah?"

What am I, the buffer for cranky senior citizens with no filter?

"Yeah." She leans across the table to whisper, "Would you like to take a trip to Vegas with me tomorrow?"

My jaw drops.

6

———

Galena

The words just flew out of my mouth. Before I can explain how his kindness and respect toward Mrs. Ellis made me think he'd be great with my grandparents, who are sticklers for manners, the waiter arrives with our food.

My mouth waters looking at all the food and that shake. It's a chocolate-shake kind of day. I barely ate today since I was so nervous about my wedding day. Now I'm taking charge of my life, starting with chocolate shakes.

The waiter chats with Levi, and even though I clearly shocked him with my invitation to Vegas, Levi still manages to be his warm and friendly self. He's great with people. Unlike myself. I'm better with numbers, though my nieces bring out a playful side I rarely indulged in before they were born.

I slurp some chocolate shake as the waiter tells Levi about a concern his mom has about wildlife that keeps knocking over their garbage cans. They're not sure if it's raccoons or feral cats. Summerdale isn't exactly a hotbed of criminal activity.

I take a big bite of burger and chew. It's not so crazy to invite Levi to Vegas, I assure myself. Let's look at the facts—I already booked the flight, hotel, and rental car, and I really want to see Grandmom and Grandpop. Why hold back? Just because my wedding was cancelled doesn't mean a honeymoon in Vegas should go to waste. Right?

Well, not exactly a honeymoon now. A platonic friend trip? I could always ask one of my girl friends in that case, couldn't I? Okay, Galena, let's be honest here. Levi is handsome with his beard and muscles. More than handsome. He's sexy in a way that makes my entire body heat and brings tingles down south, which has never happened with any guy before. Galena 2.0 is ready to experience more. At least more than scheduled Saturday nine a.m. sex.

Wow. My Saturday mornings just opened up. I can get so much more done now. Maybe I can go for a morning run around the lake. That would be much nicer than using the treadmill at the end of the day.

The moment the waiter leaves, Levi leans across the table. "Are you serious about Vegas?"

The intensity of his stare and his proximity raise goosebumps on my arms. I suddenly feel like I'm inviting him on a sexcapade. Me! Ha-ha. Maybe I am.

Galena 2.0 would go for it. What happens in Vegas stays in Vegas…

I grab my cloth napkin and put it in my lap, suddenly nervous. I've never invited a guy on a sexcapade before. "Yes, I'm serious. Everything's all arranged, and I don't want it to go to waste."

"Why me?"

I roll the edge of my napkin back and forth. I can't let him know I'm thinking all these lusty thoughts. I'm shocked at myself. I've never been a lusty-minded person before. "Mrs. Ellis says you're a fine young man, a great rule follower, and very responsible. You're perfect grandparent material."

He looks out the window, his lips pressed in a flat line. I'm not sure if he's thinking hard about it, or if he took offense to being grandparent material. Maybe I went too far in the nonlusty direction. Should I add this is a no-strings situation?

I was about to marry someone else today. Obviously I'm not ready to jump into a relationship.

He keeps looking out the window as he says, "You put a lot of stock in Mrs. Ellis's judgment considering you just met her."

And I barely know you. Am I crazy, or am I finally acting sanely? A passionless marriage would've been a life sentence.

I bluster on since I'm in this far. "Mrs. Ellis strikes me as a woman who speaks her mind, and she clearly adores her great-granddaughter. She seems like a good person; therefore, I can trust her judgment."

He's quiet, so I go with a more direct approach, even though it's tough for me to share squishy inner-feeling stuff. I've always been private and reserved. "And I think you're great." My voice cracks. I want to add he's sexy too, but I'm breathless as he turns to me, his brown eyes warming, a slow sexy smile forming on his gorgeous face. My stomach flutters. *That's new.* I thought stomach flutters only happened with a guy in the romance novels my sister reads. I may have read a few out of curiosity.

Our gazes lock for an electric moment. My lips part, my heartbeat thudding in my ears. I can't recall if he agreed to go to Vegas. I can't think of much of anything at the moment.

He leans across the table and gestures me closer. I lean forward, my breath hitching. His voice drops to a husky register that sends a hot shiver down my spine. "I'm there."

I lean back, alarmed at all the body sensations I'm experiencing—butterflies in my stomach, hot shivers, tingling nerve endings. It's like I'm experiencing a whole new body, fully alive after a long half-awake existence.

God, I hope he doesn't notice all that. I babble on to distract him. "It's just that I have a honeymoon in Vegas already planned, and it was partly to visit my grandparents, who live there. I leave tomorrow, so—"

"Galena, you don't have to convince me. I'm in."

I wiggle in my seat, energy surging through me. This is really happening. Galena 2.0 has taken charge. The hell with being a jilted bride. Now I get a sexcapade, and I don't have to disappoint Grandmom and Grandpop by not visiting. I nearly slap my forehead. I can't believe I thought of those two things at the same time. Conservative grandparents and sexcapade should never go together. I smile to myself at my silly thoughts. But they're expecting to meet Kevin. I haven't told them the wedding is off yet. God, I can't go through the wretched story again. Tomorrow is soon enough. I'll tell them in person and introduce Levi as a friend. Which he is. They don't need to know the sexy details.

A whole week in Vegas. I see now that I may have missed the potential sin factor in sin city. Levi puts it front and center. Adrenaline races through me. I feel like I could sprint all the way to Vegas right now. And that's more than two thousand miles! My heart is racing. I really need to calm down. How am I actually going to see this through?

I clutch the napkin in my lap. "Just so we're clear, I'm not ready to start anything—"

"Absolutely. I could use a break, and Vegas sounds perfect."

We smile at each other. My heartrate slows marginally. He understands it's a no-strings situation. Of course he does. He knows I was just left at the altar. *Wow. I'm really doing this.*

He shakes his head. "This is not how I expected my day to go."

"How about my day?"

We laugh and go back to eating dinner. I'm starving and finish my burger quickly while Levi eats chicken parmigiano and deals with random people stopping by the table to talk to him about town concerns. He's polite, but tells them to please call or email during office hours because he's off duty. They don't even get mad. Most people glance at me and give him an understanding smile. They probably think we're on a date. Before I was concerned about town gossip, but I tell myself it's okay. It's not like Kevin's tuned in to the town grapevine. And I'm enjoying being with Levi too much to feel bad about it.

I finish eating and look around the restaurant. It's a cute historic place with what looks like original post and beam ceilings.

"You've got four fries left," Levi points out. "You're not going to finish your meal?"

"I'm full. I usually finish ninety percent."

"Why not one hundred percent?"

"Because that's when I get full."

The hint of a smile crosses his face before he goes back to his dinner.

After a few moments, I feel the need to clarify. "Unless the restaurant serves an extra-large portion, and then I eat half."

He hides another smile by wiping his mouth with a napkin. His plate is clean now. Guess he's a member of the clean-plate club. "Interesting. So you planned your honeymoon around visiting your grandparents? Sexy."

He's teasing me, and I get how unsexy it sounds. Worse, it was all my idea. Kevin thought we could both take the weekend off work to celebrate our wedding with a movie marathon at home. Not that I don't love movie marathons. I just thought we should mark the occasion of our marriage with something special. And I missed my grandparents. I haven't seen them in a year.

"It made sense at the time," I mutter.

"I'm betting it was your ex who made it seem like the way to go since he's such an uninspiring tame guy."

That makes me feel so much better, even though I planned the entire trip. Levi sees the potential Galena 2.0 in me—a woman who longs for passion and excitement. Not just with a guy. I'm taking a new lease on a life full of excitement. My old ways didn't get me to a great place, after all.

"What are your grandparents like?" he asks.

I blink a few times, suddenly realizing I'll need a good story about Levi. They're not stupid. And I've never had a guy friend before.

"They're great," I say. "Kind of traditional. They weren't

happy that I was living with Kevin before marriage, even though it made sense to share the cost of housing."

"Uh-huh, sure. Save on rent."

I pause at the sarcasm. I consider explaining I was always spending the night at Kevin's place, so it was more convenient to move in, but do I really want to rehash my failed relationship with Levi? No, so I keep talking about my grandparents. "And they're really big on manners. Your manners are great, by the way." I'm rambling because the more I gaze into his sparkling brown eyes, the more every nerve ending tingles. I've never been so aware of all my body is doing before.

"Thanks. So your traditional grandparents chose Las Vegas to retire?"

"Just because they're traditional doesn't mean they don't like to have fun. Grandpop loves poker. Grandmom loves the slots, even though I explained that the odds don't make sense." Their happy smiles come to mind. They were ready to welcome my new husband with open arms, even though they didn't approve of us living together first. They love me unconditionally.

I sip my water. "The thing is, they're expecting to meet my husband for the first time. I sorta kept Kevin separate from my family since they didn't approve of us living together, and he didn't really want to go to family functions anyway." I take a deep breath. "I'm not asking you to pretend to be my husband, of course. We'll just say you're a friend. Could we, uh, maybe say you're gay?"

His brows shoot up. "Your traditional grandparents would be okay with a gay guy?"

"For sure. Their son, my uncle, is gay, and they never blinked an eye. They say that's the way he came into the world, and he's honoring his Maker by being true to himself."

"Progressive and traditional. Can't wait to meet them."

"So can you be my gay friend?"

He gives me a wry look. "No."

"Then what should I say about you? Do *not* tell them

we're sharing a hotel room. It has two queen-sized beds, but still…they might get the wrong idea." *The sexcapade idea. Naughty Galena shacking up with a guy before marriage again.* It occurs to me I could say Levi booked his own hotel room, but I hate lying.

He reaches across the table and squeezes my hand. A jolt runs up my arm at the contact despite the soothing tone in his voice. "Let's just play it by ear. Think of it as an adventure. Isn't that what the new Galena would do?"

I stare at his larger hand enveloping mine. So warm and tingly. "Galena 2.0."

He releases my hand and smiles at me. "We just broke Mrs. Ellis's rule for no unnecessary touching." He glances around. "Good thing her chaperone spies aren't here."

I laugh. He's awesome at keeping things light and easy. "I'll pay for your ticket. Hopefully we can get you on the same flight."

"I've got it. I've been saving for my next adventure. If I can't get on the same flight, I'll just meet up with you some-where. It's all good."

We smile at each other, and my chest warms, my entire body tingling. I'm suddenly sure I did the right thing inviting him along. I don't think I've ever had so many highs and lows in one day.

Galena 2.0 approves.

∼

Levi

I took a later flight than Galena. She had the first flight out in the morning, so I'm three hours behind her. She's picking me up at the airport. I wonder what we'll do first. Hit the casino, go to one of those all-you-can-eat buffets, or maybe get settled in at the hotel? I'd be lying if I said I didn't see the potential here. It's Vegas. Things happen, especially with the chemistry we have. I felt it, and I know she did too. I could see it in her eyes, in the flush of her skin, in the sound of her sexy, breathy voice.

Of course I can't forget her ex waiting for her at home. For me, this thing with Galena isn't a hookup situation. She's the first woman in a long time I'm excited about. The last thing I want is to be her rebound guy. I've been that guy before with my ex Alissa, not knowing she was using me to get over someone, until it was over suddenly, and I was left with a broken heart while she skipped happily away to the next guy she actually liked.

I'm getting ahead of myself. Fact is, Galena liked me so much after just one day she invited me to spend a week with her. Baxter liked her too. He didn't bark or turn his back on her. He turns his back on me when he's mad, like when I take him to the vet or the kennel. Luckily for Baxter, Adam and Kayla are dog sitting for the week. I'm sure he'll have a great time with Tank and Simba. That's who he's always escaping to see.

I spot Galena at baggage claim, where we agreed to meet. Her dark hair is pulled back from her face in a low ponytail, emphasizing her round cheeks and full lips. Cute and sexy. My gaze trails to the long row of buttons running down the center of her light blue dress with a pattern of small roses. I imagine unbuttoning that dress, slowly revealing more skin… Too soon.

Follow her lead. She could be wrecked on the inside from her ex, even though she looks amazing and sexy on the outside.

I raise a hand toward her. "Galena!"

She smiles and bounces on the balls of her feet. "You made it!"

I close the distance, tempted to hug her and swing her around. I kiss her cheek instead, careful not to bump her large, black-framed glasses. "Great to see you."

She pushes her glasses up her nose, a faint pink to her cheeks. "You too. What's it been, a whole day?"

"Feels like a week."

She giggles, and my hopes soar. She's happy to see me. "Did you check a bag?"

"Nope. Just my carry-on."

"Great. Let's go. I already got the rental car and checked in at the hotel."

The heat slaps me the moment we step outside. It must be a hundred degrees. Palm trees against a cloudless blue sky. Cool. I've only ever seen palm trees in pictures. In fact, I've never left the Northeast. Why haven't I traveled more? There always seemed more to do for work. Even when I was a history teacher before the mayor gig, I worked summers for the historical homestead nearby and volunteered on various town committees. My sense of responsibility toward Summerdale kept me tethered there with only the occasional road trip.

I still can't believe I left work for a week. I told the town clerk I'd deal with all nonemergency issues when I return. Hopefully, there's no emergencies. The last emergency was a hurricane that took out the power for a week. Weather report looked good back home last I checked.

Galena asks me about my flight as we walk to the short-term parking lot.

"Considering it was my first flight, I'm just happy we landed safe and sound."

She grabs my arm. "Oh my God, you've never flown before? And you did it by yourself? My first flight I held Grandmom's hand for takeoff and landing. Are you okay?"

I laugh. "Yes, I'm okay. It was great. I'm all about making the most of every moment, ready for new experiences."

"Just don't do anything too risky. Like jumping from an airplane."

"Nah. Too many people depending on me to take life-or-death risks."

A short time later, she stops next to a white Jeep Wrangler and opens the back for my bags. "I've never driven a Jeep before. I thought it'd be fun."

"Cool." I stow my duffel bag and backpack in the Jeep, shut the back, and get into the passenger side.

Galena starts the car, and we're off. I look out the window and find myself smiling at the foreign-looking scenery. Look at all the sandy beige-colored highway dividers and buildings. A desert color palette. We're not even on the strip yet. Right after I booked my flight last night and took care of work and Baxter arrangements, I started researching Las Vegas. I'm beyond excited to be here and experience everything.

"What hotel are we at?" I ask.

"The Venetian Resort."

"That's the one with the canals and that bridge, right? Like a mini Venice."

"Yes, but I mostly booked it because it was rated the most romantic hotel in Las Vegas. I did my research."

She doesn't sound all that excited about romantic stuff. I figure it couldn't hurt our situation. "Works for me."

"Are you tired?"

"No, I'm sorta buzzed right now. Excited to be here."

"Great. If you could just give me a little background on you, so it doesn't sound like we just met in front of my grandparents, that would be helpful."

I glance around and realize we're heading toward a suburban area. "Are we visiting your grandparents right now?"

"Yes, they can't wait to see me and my, uh, friend."

"You didn't tell them I was your gay friend, did you?" That could be a major problem down the line. Let's start things on the right foot.

She makes a right turn. "This car is fun to drive."

"What did you tell them about me?"

She pulls the visor down, adjusts her glasses, and glances at me before focusing back on the road. "Not much. That's why I need some background on you."

"Define not much."

"I didn't say you were gay."

"Okay, so what do you want to know?"

"Where you grew up, a little about your family, college, career. Give me the highlights."

I decide to be more open about my life than I usually am because I'm here to take risks, even the kind that require the courage to be vulnerable. Maybe hitting thirty triggered Levi 2.0. Ha. "Grew up in Summerdale. Dad died when I was seven and my sister, Avery, was five. Everyone in Summerdale helped our family out, stopping by with a casserole or taking me and Avery someplace when Mom had to work. It was a good place to grow up, and I'm glad to give back now as mayor."

"I'm sorry for your loss."

I swallow over the lump in my throat. Somehow it never gets easier to talk about. "Thanks. Dad died when he was thirty-four, only four years older than me now. He had a heart abnormality no one knew about. It's really made me think about life and how I'm living mine. That's why I'm open to new experiences like getting a Harley and taking off to Vegas on a moment's notice. I'm grabbing life with both hands. You never know how much time you have left."

"Exploring your wild side."

"It was there all along."

She glances over at me with concern in her eyes. "It sounds like you think you're going to be like your dad. Have you seen a doctor?"

"Yeah, I'm fine. But part of me can't help thinking I'm on the clock."

"Aren't we all?"

I still, her words hitting home. "Huh. Guess that's true." My impending sense of doom eases. It's not something I ever talk about, but it's driven most of my decisions ever since I hit thirty. Living life to the fullest is what we all should do, not just me.

"Is your family still local?" she asks.

"Mom's in Georgia now, and Avery's with her husband in Germany. He's in the Air Force. No kids yet."

"So we both have sisters in common. Mine's older, and

yours is younger. You mentioned you're thirty. I'm twenty-six. Oh, and my sister is Izzy. My nieces—"

"Amelia and Grace."

She glances at me, her eyes lighting up. "You remember!"

"It was just yesterday you told me all about them."

"Right! So much has happened in such a short time. Okay, we're off to a great start. What did your parents do for work?"

"Mom was a high school English teacher before she retired. She dreamed of writing a novel, but never had time. Dad was vice principal of a high school in another district, who dreamed of one day moving to Costa Rica and running an ecoresort. He grew up in Summerdale."

Mom still never wrote that novel, and Dad's dream was cut short. No wonder I have this urgency to do something cool before I run out of time. If only I knew what that cool thing is. All I know is I need new experiences to find out.

"Does your mom write books now that she's retired?" Galena asks.

"Nope. She plays mah-jongg and goes to book club. That's it."

"I guess that could be fun too. I grew up in the Bronx, New York, in a crowded apartment with my parents, sister, and grandparents. Izzy and I got the sofa bed in the living room. Mom runs a nonprofit for the arts, and Dad was a mailman before he retired. I went to a magnet high school for math and science and from there went to college, majoring in statistics, went on for my master's degree, and now I'm a biostatistician. I love my job. Do you love your job?"

I think about that. "I like it, but I don't feel passionate about it."

"Oh, well, liking it is good. Not everyone feels passionate about their job. Mine just happens to be a perfect fit for what I love to do. I get to play with spreadsheets and mathematical models all day long. And I know my work helps a lot of people. I give the stamp of approval on medical treatments or decline them if it's not statistically significant for effectiveness."

"That's great. Anything else you want to know about me?"

"What was your major in college?"

"History."

"Interesting. What do you do with that?"

"I was a history teacher at a private high school for a few years, but then the mayor position opened up, and I went for that instead. I wasn't loving teaching, honestly."

"But you're such a people person!"

"I didn't have much patience for teens who couldn't care less about history and cared more about their phones. Their entitled attitudes rubbed me the wrong way. Maybe it was just the school, but I was ready to come back to Summerdale. And Mom was ready to retire and move to a warmer climate, so the timing worked out for me to buy our family home from her."

"Wow, full circle. I'd never want to move back to my old apartment. Not that I could. My parents moved down south for warmer weather too. Florida."

She pulls into a subdivision of beige single-story homes with a sign out front that reads Sunny Horizons. "It's a fifty-five-and-up active-adult community. They have a pool, tennis court, golf course, and fitness center. The real reason my grandparents chose this one is how close it is to the casinos. There's a shuttle bus too. They want to go frequently without worrying about parking."

She glances at me. "I should probably mention I didn't exactly tell my grandparents you'd be here."

"You didn't? I thought they knew since we did the whole get-our-stories-straight thing."

"Well, they *will* know when I introduce you, so it's good we know each other's story."

"So they're expecting Kevin, and I'm about to walk into grandparent outrage in approximately two minutes."

"How could they be outraged with someone like you with

all your great people skills?"

I open my mouth to argue that she should've told them, but she barrels on.

"I'll introduce you as my friend Levi and then break the news that Kevin's out of the picture. That way they won't ask too many questions. They would never ask me a lot of personal questions in front of company. I just don't want to rehash all that, you know? I want to enjoy this trip and not think about it until I get back."

I let out a breath. *What choice do I have?* "Okay, you know them best."

She turns left and slows down for a golf cart with a group of elderly women wearing brightly colored visors. "You're not mad?"

"It's your family. I'm just along for the ride. Can we hit the casino after this?"

"I really hope you're not one of those slots players. Mathematically—"

"This trip is all about fun, even if it's not mathematically reasonable. You did rent the Jeep for a fun ride."

She looks sheepish. "I actually swapped for it when I got here. I rented a sensible Camry."

"Why do you look guilty?"

"The Jeep was more money, and it seems like such a guilty pleasure to drive a fun car instead of a sensible one. I didn't even ask about the fuel efficiency."

"Horror!"

She laughs. "I know!"

"No guilty pleasure on this trip. Only pleasure." My voice sounds husky, a hint at potential.

I hear her sharp intake of breath as she tightens her grip on the steering wheel, her knuckles turning white. She pulls into her grandparents' driveway and turns off the car, staring straight ahead. "Right. Pleasure trip. That's what a honey— vacation should be." She turns to me. "Not a honey vacation just a vacation."

My lips curve up. "Anyone ever tell you you're cute as a

button?"

Her lips part. "No. Anyone ever tell you you're the sexiest man they've ever met?" She slaps a hand over her mouth.

This is going to be interesting.

7

I step into my grandparents' house and immediately want to make a quick exit. The living room is filled with older guests I've never met for a party in my honor. There's congratulations balloons in silver and pink, along with a huge congratulations sign. Over in the dining room on my right, I spot a table groaning with food with a white-tiered wedding cake in the center.

I probably should've broken the bad news earlier. *Understatement.* I had no idea they'd throw a party. Guess my family's on board once we put a ring on it.

"Congratulations!" Grandmom exclaims, wrapping me in a hug.

I breathe in her familiar floral scent, my mind racing. I pull back to look at her kindly face with the smile lines by her brown eyes. She wears cat's-eye glasses, her gray hair falling to her shoulders. "Grandmom, who are these people?"

She gestures toward them, smiling. "Our neighbors. We've been so lucky with the people on our cul-de-sac. I know you missed out on a reception with the elopement, so we wanted to throw you a little party. Are you surprised?"

"Very."

Grandpop beams at me. He's looking handsome in a

white button-down shirt with short sleeves, his gray hair slick with gel and parted to the side. "There's my girl." He crushes me in a hug. He's not a large man, but he's got a big heart and strong arms. "Congratulations! We were sorry to miss the ceremony, but here we are now ready to celebrate with you."

"You didn't have to—"

His dark eyes sparkle with glee. "Of course we did!"

He turns to Levi, and Levi holds out his hand to shake. Grandpop shoves Levi's hand away. "Welcome to the family!" He hugs Levi, pounding him on the back.

"Uh…" Levi starts, but then Grandmom is hugging him and welcoming him to the family too.

Grandmom smiles widely at Levi. "I'm Betsy, and this is my husband, Nick."

Grandpop grumbles, "You can call me Mr. Torres."

"Nice to meet you both," Levi says.

"Uh…" I start, but Grandmom cuts me off.

"We got you a wedding cake, and our friend Brenda is excellent with the photos. She promised to take some of the traditional shots we missed. You must be hungry. I'll go get the lasagna from the oven."

She hustles off, and Grandpop immediately starts introducing us to several seventy-something couples with vibrant energy like my grandparents. Hearty congratulations follow, and then Mrs. Nuckowski, a petite woman with jet-black hair with a white streak starting at her forehead all the way to the back, shows us a gift table in the back of the room with an assortment of envelopes and large wrapped gifts. I missed seeing that before with all the guests. My stomach does a slow roll.

Mrs. Nuckowski gestures to the table of gifts. "Just a few things that might be helpful in setting up your home together. I can have them shipped to you so you don't have to take them on the plane. I get a discount on shipping through my son's business."

"This is too much," I whisper, staring at the gifts. I'm guessing the large boxes are appliances or dishes. Household stuff. Kevin and I already bought that stuff, though now that we're separating, maybe it'll be good to have.

I inwardly cringe and glance at Levi, who smiles at me. I send him a telepathic message, *We can't take wedding gifts under false pretenses!*

He takes my hand and gives it a squeeze. A rush of warmth shoots straight up my arm. Even when I'm distressed, my body's reacting to him with all its new sensations.

Mrs. Nuckowski smiles kindly. "We know what it's like when you're newlyweds just starting out. Congratulations, you two!"

"Thank you," Levi answers for us.

I'm speechless, only managing a small wave as she walks off, mingling with the other guests.

I stare at the assortment of gifts.

Levi nudges his arm with mine. "Seems like you should've mentioned the real deal before we left New York."

I turn to him. "I had no idea they were going to do all this."

"Too late now. Just go with it." He leans down to my ear. "It makes them happy."

We turn, and a flash goes off. A woman with dyed red hair wearing a black halter-style jumpsuit just took our picture.

She wiggles her fingers in a small wave. "I'm Brenda. Your grandparents asked me to take pictures. Don't mind me. Just enjoy yourselves."

Grandmom gestures to us. "Come and eat. You must be hungry after your long trip."

Levi takes my hand in his, sending a jolt of energy straight up my arm as he walks with me to the dining room.

Grandmom hands me a plate. "I made all your favorites."

I take the plate and, for the first time, take a good look at the spread—lasagna, mac and cheese, green beans with slivered almonds, red Jell-O with fruit cocktail in it, even celery stuffed with pimiento cheese. All my childhood favorites. Hot tears sting my eyes. Grandmom catered especially to me.

"It's an emotional time," she whispers. "Enjoy it."

After I fill my plate, I join Levi in the living room. He's sitting in one of two upholstered navy floral chairs positioned next to each other.

I turn to him, and a flash goes off nearby.

"No rings?" photographer Brenda asks.

"They're being engraved," Levi says smoothly.

My head whips toward him. How deep are we going to get here with the lying? He widens his eyes at me. He's enjoying himself too much.

"Anyone willing to let the bride and groom borrow their wedding rings?" Brenda asks. "Just for the pictures. Theirs are being engraved."

Everyone, literally everyone, including my grandparents, wants to help. Then they all start fighting over who's going to be the one to give us the rings.

"She's my granddaughter!" Grandmom says, yanking her wedding band off and thrusting it into my hand.

Grandpop does the same for Levi. The ring doesn't fit. "Harry, get over here!" Grandpop yells. "We need someone with big hands." He smiles at Levi. "I have piano-playing hands."

"So you do."

With that, Grandpop goes over to his electronic keyboard on the other side of the room and starts playing "At Last" by Etta James. One of his neighbors joins him by the keyboard and sings quite beautifully.

Levi's ring is secured, and he turns toward Brenda. I paste on a smile as she takes our picture.

"Get closer," Brenda urges. "Pretend you like each other."

Levi laughs and puts his arm around me. I put my arm around his waist, even though I'm not used to public displays of affection. My cheeks burn as I sense all eyes on us.

Brenda snaps a bunch of pictures. "Okay, go back to your meal. We'll do the cake slicing after this."

I go back to eating. Levi does too. People keep coming over to congratulate us and ask us about life back in

Summerdale. This is Levi's field of expertise, and he holds court telling everyone about the quirky people in town—a tamale-delivering mailman, a grocery store owner who resembles Santa, and Mrs. Ellis, who everyone secretly calls General Joan, but who thinks of herself as Cupid. I laugh. I actually met her.

Then he starts sharing about all the festivals for every season, all the special occasions that bring people together, and I find myself enthralled with a town I've barely begun to explore. I've been all work and no fun.

"We'll have to go with you to visit these two!" Brenda tells Grandmom.

"The more the merrier," Grandmom declares. "I'm just so happy Galena found someone special. Her sister was not so lucky." Her lips purse.

Grandpop's jaw clenches. "Let's not talk about him. He's not worth the breath."

My sister's cheating husband denied it all the way until she caught him in the middle of the act in his car parked on a side street from their apartment. Real classy.

Grandpop gestures to Levi. "Let's talk for a minute out on the patio."

My stomach lurches. Here comes a man-to-man conversation all about treating me right, which Levi shouldn't have to endure. "Wait for me."

"Stay here, sweetheart," Grandpop says.

"But—"

"It's okay," Levi says. "I was finished eating anyway."

He walks through the back door with my grandfather. My appetite disappears.

Grandmom swoops by to take Levi's empty plate.

I stand with my plate. "I'll help with the dishes."

"You didn't finish your mac 'n cheese. Did you fill up on food on the plane? I heard they weren't feeding people much these days. When we flew out here, they only gave us pretzels."

"I filled up on your delicious lasagna."

I follow her to the kitchen. She rinses Levi's plate. I can see Levi and my grandfather through the kitchen window. They're standing under the shade of the patio cover. Grandpop's doing all the talking with a stern expression on his face while Levi listens intently. I guess as mayor he gets an earful from a lot of people. This time it's probably a lecture about staying faithful in our marriage, which is so undeserved. My poor fake husband.

Grandmom takes the plate I'm holding. "Relax, we both like Kevin. He's so warm and friendly. We're pleasantly surprised after your sister reported back that she didn't care for him."

I want to spill my guts, but I can't tear my eyes off Grandpop and Levi. I should go rescue him.

Levi nods, says something, and shakes Grandpop's hand. Levi looks up, catching my eye, and my breath hitches. He's a gorgeous man. The kind of guy your family actually likes. Husband material? Goosebumps break out on my arms. I can only imagine how Kevin would've acted at this party. Probably spent most of his time on his phone, barely listening to those around him. I have to stop comparing the two of them. Levi is nothing like Kevin.

He's nothing like any man I've ever met.

Levi holds the back door for Grandpop, who walks into the kitchen and announces, "Good talk!"

"Cake time!" Brenda says, appearing in the kitchen.

"Let's go," Grandmom says, shooing us out.

Levi takes my hand and walks out with me to the dining room. I'm dying to ask what Grandpop said to him. Surprisingly, Levi doesn't seem fazed in the least. Maybe it was just a few innocent questions. No. This is Grandpop. The same man who tracked down Izzy's cheating husband and yelled in his face. I heard about it from the neighbors. Anyhoo…I owe Levi big time after this.

We're hustled over to one side of the dining room table by the cake while the guests all gather on the other side to watch. Grandmom hands me the cake slicer.

"Both of you hold it," Brenda says, camera at the ready.

Levi's big warm hand envelops mine. Heat rushes through my entire body. He's close; we're practically cheek to cheek.

"Ready?" he asks me.

And it suddenly feels like he's asking me if I'm ready for more with him. Adrenaline races through me. "Ready."

We slice through the bottom layer together. I help slide the slice onto a plate with a shaky hand.

"Feed it to each other!" Grandmom calls.

"Shove it in his face!" someone yells.

"Oh, that's not necessary," I say, feeling like the world's biggest fraud. What am I even doing slicing wedding cake with Levi? We're not even together.

A forkful of cake appears in front of my mouth. Levi's eyes are warm on mine. "It's tradition."

I open my mouth, and he feeds me the cake very nicely. It's vanilla with buttercream frosting. Delicious. I so owe him for making this look good.

I take a forkful and hold it up to him, whispering, "We can do anything you want after this."

"Anything?"

My heart lurches at his husky tone, a flutter low in my belly, and a lower ache making me realize just what he's asking. I feed him cake instead of answering. His smoldering eyes are locked on mine. Flashes go off, and I'm barely aware of them, caught in the intense heat building between us.

"Kiss your bride!" Brenda yells.

Everyone claps and starts chanting, "Kiss the bride, kiss the bride."

Levi checks in with me, his lips curving up. The peer pressure is killing me. My aches and flutters and tingles are killing me. That's it. We *have* to kiss.

He slowly leans down toward me, and I give him a quick peck before turning to the crowd, smiling, even as my lips tingle from just a peck.

Brenda looks disappointed. "I didn't get a good shot. Do it again. Longer this time."

I glance nervously at Levi.

The peer pressure kicks in again. "Kiss, kiss, kiss."

I take a deep breath and turn to the crowd, about to confess all, when Levi's large hand cups my jaw, turning me toward him. He dips me suddenly over his arm, his lips covering mine. I'm so shocked by the move I don't even squeak. His lips are warm and firm, expertly moving over mine. My body ignites, sensation racing through my limbs. I'm only dimly aware of applause.

He brings me back upright. I stare at him, shaken by all I feel. He smooths his hair back, smiling, but also looking a little shocked. I didn't know a kiss could feel like that. Like I lost my bearing in the world, clinging to a man's body like it's the only thing tethering me to Earth. *This* man's body.

Grandmom starts slicing cake efficiently. "You two can go ahead and have your fun after this. I'm sure you want some alone time."

Levi grins at me. "You did say I could do anything I wanted after this."

My jaw drops. He's not going to say something dirty in front of my grandparents and their friends, is he?

Grandmom titters but doesn't comment, moving along to give out cake to her friends.

"Uh," I manage, staring at the cake in front of me, still shaken from that incredible kiss.

"Let's go to the casino and play slots," Levi says.

My head whips toward his. "I need to explain the house advantage to you."

"You said *anything*." He calls over to my grandmother, "Betsy, I hear you're a whiz at slots. Why don't you and Mr. Torres come along? There's room for you in the Jeep."

Grandmom whoops. "Nick, we're going to the slots with Kevin and Galena after this! Hey, everyone, join us!"

I *really* need to tell them the truth. I swear I will as soon as we get time alone.

"You're all very welcome. Drinks on me!" Levi says, spreading his arms wide.

My heart kicks harder. I think I'm halfway in love.

The party's over, and Levi and I walk over to the Jeep. Grandmom and Grandpop are gathering their things for our casino trip. Apparently, they both have lucky shirts, and Grandmom has a lucky hat. They also wanted to gather all the quarters they could find in the house for the slots. Their friends are all heading out for their cars.

"I'll tell them the truth in the car," I say, waving bye to a nice couple whose names I forgot.

"Better than at our wedding reception," Levi replies with a wink.

"This isn't funny."

"It's kinda funny. Anyway, I had fun pretending. I've never been a groom before."

I want to ask him if that kiss was pretend for him. I've never been kissed that way before; never felt an instant rush of desire just from a kiss. "Which part of being a groom did you like best?"

His lips curve up in a sexy smile that makes my heart beat faster.

"We're ready to go, lovebirds!" Grandmom exclaims.

They hurry over to us, wearing matching red Hawaiian shirts. Grandmom has a leopard-patterned bucket hat with a large black purse that I assume is full of quarters. Guess it won't be hard to find them at the casino.

"Nice rental," Grandpop says appreciatively.

I lift my palms. "Wait. Before we go, I need to tell you guys something."

"What is it, sweetheart?" Grandmom asks.

"Kevin and I broke up."

She glances up at Levi standing loyally by my side, and whispers loudly, "Then what's he doing here?"

I gesture toward him. "This is Levi. I'm sorry I didn't explain earlier. I was surprised by the party, and it just snowballed from there."

Grandpop studies Levi. "You know, I did wonder about you when you walked in. You're not Galena's usual sciencey type."

Grandmom and Grandpop exchange an amused look.

"Actually, I'm not sciencey at all," Levi says. "I majored in history, taught it at a high school for a few years, and now I'm on my second term as the mayor of Summerdale, where Galena recently moved."

"And when did you two meet?" Grandmom asks.

"Two months ago," Levi says.

Grandmom and Grandpop exchange a significant look at this.

Grandmom turns to me. "Galena, last week when you called, you were about to marry Kevin, but you were also seeing Levi for the last two months, and now you decided to be with him. Did I get that right?"

I wave my hands in front of me. "No, no, no. I didn't cheat on Kevin. You know that's not like me."

"Sorry," Grandmom says. "I'm just confused about Levi here. You two look so happy together, and the kiss at the party looked like true love's kiss."

Grandpop nods.

My face flushes hot, and I blurt out the rest, "I was only with Kevin. I planned to marry him all the way until he dumped me at the altar by text." My voice chokes.

"Oh, honey." Grandmom wraps me in a hug. "What a cowardly move he pulled."

"Your sister was right," Grandpop announces grimly. "She knows a rat when she smells him."

Grandmom pulls away and rubs my arm. "I hope Kevin walks off a cliff. He stole two years of prime dating time from you when you could've been searching for a better man. One who would give us grandbabies. Ooh, if I met him right now, I'd give him a piece of my mind."

Grandpop grabs me in a hug and kisses the top of my head.

I gesture to the Jeep. "Should we go to the casino now?"

"Yes, let's go," Grandmom says.

I unlock the Jeep, and Levi opens the back door for Grandmom. She smiles at him. "Thank you."

He goes to open my door, but I'm already there. Instead he walks around to the other side of the car with Grandpop, who's talking to him in a low voice. Now what's he lecturing Levi about?

After I get in the car, Grandpop gives me directions to their favorite casino. It's quiet in the back seat for a few minutes. I'm waiting for the Levi questions. Instead Grandmom starts fretting about me to Grandpop.

"It's not like her to rush into something with a man," Grandmom says. "She's always been very careful, analyzing all the pros and cons. So what's he doing here?"

"I have to admit it's not like her, but who can predict love? Remember the first day we met?"

"Oh, Nick, of course I do."

There's a rustle of clothing as they reach for each other and kiss. I glance at Levi, who's fighting back a laugh.

"What's your last name, Levi?" Grandmom asks once they come up for air.

"Appleton."

"Appleton's a good last name," Grandpop says. "Solid."

I bet Grandmom Googles him when she gets home. She's very savvy on the computer.

"Where are you staying, Levi?" Grandmom asks.

Levi glances at me before saying, "At The Venetian."

"That's where Galena is staying," Grandmom says. "Galena, I understand love at first sight, that's exactly how it was for me and your grandfather, but I really hope you're not shacking up with another man. Didn't you learn your lesson the first time?"

I grit my teeth. Shacking up is how she says getting naked

with another man. It applies to everything from hookups to living together. All the same to her.

Grandpop chimes in, "Your grandmom and I dated for six weeks before we were married."

"A whirlwind romance in the proper order," Grandmom says. "No shenanigans."

I desperately want to roll my eyes. Not hard to wait for sex when you only date for six weeks.

"Married more than fifty years now," Grandpop says.

"Congratulations," Levi says. "It's great to see two people still so in love after all those years."

An awkward silence falls. Every muscle in my body tenses because I'm trapped in a car for what promises to be a long, embarrassing lecture. I'm sure they've got more to say.

Grandpop clears his throat. "Levi, I'd like to know your intentions toward Galena."

I stare straight ahead even as heat burns my cheeks. I bet Levi's sorry he invited my grandparents to the casino with us.

"Honorable, sir," Levi says. "Today's the first day of a new relationship for us."

My jaw gapes. I can't believe he said that. Does he really believe it? I thought we were on the same page that this was just a no-strings week of fun. I grip the steering wheel tighter.

My grandparents are quiet for a moment.

I turn onto the highway and hit the accelerator.

"They're like us, Nick," Grandmom whispers loudly to Grandpop.

"Mmm-hmm."

"So, Levi, how do you feel about kids?" Grandmom asks.

"Grandmom!"

"What? Kevin didn't want kids, so no kids. Now you're starting something new, though it's quick, I understand sometimes love happens that way. Now I want to know if I'm going to have more grandbabies."

I glance at Levi, thoroughly embarrassed. "You don't have to answer that." I glance toward the back seat. "This entire conversation is way beyond appropriate."

"Levi, why don't you stay with us?" Grandpop asks. "We have a pull-out sofa."

"He's staying at the hotel with me," I say.

Levi turns toward the back seat. "I'm glad to finally get the chance to know your amazing, beautiful, smart granddaughter better."

My throat tightens. Does he mean that? Or is he just trying to appease my grandparents? I've been called smart plenty of times but never amazing or beautiful.

"Did you hear that, Galena?" Grandmom asks.

I stifle a groan. "Yes, of course I heard it. He's sitting right next to me."

"So what are you going to do about it?" she asks.

I assume sexcapade isn't the right answer here.

"This one is special," Grandmom whispers loudly to Grandpop.

"We had a nice talk out back. He's a good one," Grandpop whispers back.

"You're very quiet up there, Galena," Grandmom says.

Maybe it's better to just let them believe it's a whirlwind romance. As long as Levi understands I'm not ready for anything serious, it won't hurt anyone.

"It has been a whirlwind," I say.

Levi smiles.

"Don't rush, though," Grandpop says.

"Yes, no rush," Grandmom says. "I may have gotten ahead of myself. Galena, you'll want time to heal from getting left at the altar. We don't want Levi to be nothing more than the rebound guy."

"Maybe he *is* the rebound guy," Grandpop says under his breath.

"I hope not," Grandmom whispers back.

Levi stares out the window, his jaw tight.

"Galena, what are your intentions toward Levi?" Grandpop asks.

"We like Levi," Grandmom says. "He's a mayor, he likes kids, and he respects his elders."

"And he's faithful," Grandpop says. "Right, Levi?"

"Right," Levi says flatly. Did my grandparents finally get to him?

I have no idea what to say. It seems my grandparents are already on board with Levi as my future husband and the father of my children. On day one. I can't help but wonder how they would've reacted to meeting Kevin for the first time. Would we be having this same conversation? Somehow I doubt it.

"Of course you'll need to get a separate hotel room for a proper courtship," Grandmom says. "Take things slow so Galena has time to get over her ex."

Levi continues staring straight ahead, seeming done with the conversation.

"Don't worry, Grandmom," I say. "I know the right thing to do."

Have my dirty, filthy way with the mayor of Summerdale.

Once we clear up the relationship thing. Levi can't possibly think I brought him to a week in Vegas to start something as big as a relationship. He must've just been saying that for my grandparents' benefit so they'd let up on us.

Grandmom pats my shoulder. "Good girl. I'm sure doing things in the proper order will have a much better result with this one. He's a keeper."

Ha. Proper order is out the window. I guess we're doomed to have wild sex and walk away forever with nothing but our happy memories. My chest tightens. That doesn't sound like as much fun as I thought it would.

8

Galena

The moment we get back to our hotel room, I flop face-down on the bed, my head on the silky soft pillow. I'm exhausted after hours in the casino. Grandmom, Levi, and friends all had a blast at the slots. I lost twenty bucks and retreated to the poker table with Grandpop.

The mattress across from me creaks as Levi makes himself comfortable on the other queen-sized bed. I crack an eye open. He's sitting up, leaning back against the headboard, shoes off, looking relaxed. I passed relaxed after all the shiny lights and constant din of coins hitting metal trays, slots beeping, and shouts of joy. I need absolute silence.

Levi pipes up, "So I heard there's a cool cirque show in town. You know with all the acrobatics. I've never seen them. How about dinner and a show tonight?"

I turn my head to face him. "I'm on sensory overload. I don't think I can take a show. Not even sure about dinner."

He swings his legs over to the floor and peers at me. "You've been through a lot in the last couple of days."

"Yeah, it's been a whirlwind."

His lips curve up in an irresistible smile. My heart kicks harder, which I thought exhaustion would've prevented happening. Levi just gets to me. "Your grandparents had some opinions on that. It seems they enjoyed their whirlwind romance."

I sit up, propping pillows behind me against the headboard. "That stuff you said before in the car with them, you were just saying that to get them off our backs, right?"

"No. I do think you're beautiful, smart, and amazing."

Alarm fires through me. Does he really think this is day one of a relationship? Is my first sexcapade going to fizzle before it even gets started? Not that I know exactly how to start a sexcapade. "I thought we talked about this before when we were at dinner at The Horseman Inn. I said I wasn't ready to start anything, and you said, 'Absolutely.'"

"And what did you think that meant?"

"What did *you* think?"

His eyes are intent on mine. "That it was too soon for a committed relationship for you."

I let out a breath of relief. "Exactly. I just ended a long-term relationship with the man I nearly married. Good. We're on the same page. This isn't day one of a new relationship for us."

He leans forward, resting his elbows on his knees. "So I'm your rebound guy."

"No, not exactly. I'm not using you to get over him." I reach out to squeeze his hand, but he's too far away to reach, and he doesn't meet me halfway. I drop my hand, feeling lower than low. "I hope you don't feel like I'm using you. I just thought we could have, you know, fun together."

"Define fun."

Geez, this is much harder than I thought it would be. Here we are, two single people in a hotel room, and I don't know how to get things started. He feels so far away sitting on the other bed. Should I join him there? Should I just take my clothes off? I've never been a seductress before. I don't even know how to flirt. Kevin and I had a meeting of the minds. *Don't think about him!*

"There's lots of fun activities to do in Vegas," I say lamely.

He raises his brows, looking at me expectantly. It seems

he's not the kind of guy to pounce on a woman without clarity about the parameters. Maybe he's more scientific than I thought. That would explain my instant attraction and crazy body reactions whenever he gets close.

I take a deep breath. "Like hanging by the pool with a good book."

"You don't need me for that."

I lick my lips. *Is he really going to make me spell it out?* "And taking a gondola ride through the hotel's canals. That's something I wouldn't want to do alone."

"Uh-huh. Anything else?"

I wince. "Saying it out loud sounds kinda bad, like I only see you as one thing for one purpose, but that's not true at all. I definitely can tell you're a good person, who could also be my friend."

"Friend," he echoes like it's a dirty word. "I've got plenty of friends, Galena." There's a husky tone to his voice now that makes me think he knows what I'm getting at. He just needs me to say it.

I look to the ceiling and back to him. "You seem in touch with your wild side, and I want to discover mine. Like on your Harley and—" I cough "—naked."

He cocks his head. "Then you just want no-strings sex and that's it."

"Yes!" I'm so relieved he gets it. I wasn't sure how to say it nicely.

He straightens. "Thanks for clarifying that."

This man is awesome. He gets it, and he even thanked me for making the effort to communicate clearly. I smile. "You're amazing with older people. My grandparents loved you."

He makes a face and gets out of bed, taking a tour of the living room instead of me. I thought we were about to start the fun. I hide my disappointment and scoot back down on the mattress. Just as well. I'm wiped out.

"This is the biggest hotel room I've ever stayed in," he says. We're in the honeymoon suite. There's a sunken living room with a sofa, TV, and a couple of plush chairs.

"Seven hundred fifty square feet." What can I say, I have a head for numbers, and I remember that fact from when I booked it a couple of months ago.

He takes the two steps up to the bedroom area and continues on to the bathroom. He lets out a loud whistle and steps back into the bedroom. "Marble as far as the eye can see, a soaking tub for two, and a large shower with dual spouts. Seems like a lot of opportunities for honeymoon activities." He waggles his brows, and my blood pressure skyrockets. I've never done anything in a tub or shower. Strictly the bed for naked activities.

"That would be really wild. I'm not sure how comfortable it would be though."

He smirks and returns to sit on the bed facing me. "There's luxury toiletries in there too. My sister spends a fortune for that stuff."

I roll to my side. "I wouldn't know about that." I take a deep breath, about to ask him if he wants to get naked. No, wait. I need to warm him up first. I'll ask him to take a gondola ride with me as foreplay. It's supposed to be romantic, set the mood. Somehow I can't get the words out.

I roll to my back and stare at the ceiling. "What did Grandpop say when he took you out on the patio?"

"He asked me if I'd be faithful to you, and I said yes."

I roll to my side again. "Anything else?"

"He also asked if I'd always been a one-woman guy, or if it was new for me." He pauses, a smile playing over his lips. "I told him it would be way too much work to keep multiple women happy. He laughed."

I purse my lips. "Women aren't difficult to keep happy. At least I'm not."

"Yeah, what makes you happy?"

"As long as we're not fighting over stuff, then it's good."

"That's it? Not fighting? What if you fight and make up? Couldn't it be good again after that?"

"Kevin and I never fought. It was peaceful."

"The results speak for themselves on that one. Anyway,

your grandfather's got a great sense of humor. He said he was glad I only wanted to make one woman happy; otherwise, he'd have to break my kneecaps."

I cringe. Grandpop wouldn't go that far, but he'd definitely go after a guy he felt did his granddaughter wrong.

His eyes widen. "He was kidding, right?"

"Oh yeah. For sure."

"He also asked me if I'd always try to make you happy, for better or for worse. And I told him I'd do my best."

I sigh. "You're too good. My grandparents are going to think I'm awful for dumping you."

He gets serious. "So don't dump me."

I swallow hard. "I thought we agreed to a week of fun."

He lifts his palms. "After the wedding reception we had, it feels like we're fake married already. Let's play that to the hilt. I bet honeymooners get all sorts of perks here."

"What! That's crazy."

"Crazier than pretending to be married for a wedding reception?"

"I had no idea they'd go to that much trouble."

He lifts his brows. "We passed a few wedding chapels on the way in. Just saying."

"Not funny."

He smiles, his eyes warm on mine. "Look at that, our first fight. And us only fake married one day."

My mind flashes back to the party, when Levi kissed his bride in the most dramatic way, bending me back over his arm. "Are you going to kiss the bride again?"

His voice drops to a husky tone. "Do you want me to kiss the bride again?"

A flash of heat rushes through my body at the thought. So much yes. My mouth goes dry. "I think so, yes."

"You *think* so? I'll wait until you know for sure. How about this, I'll only kiss you when someone says to kiss the bride. What are the odds of that happening again?"

I think back to the two bachelorette parties and a newlywed couple wearing a bridal veil and top hat respectively I saw earlier in the casino among lots of other couples. "Based on today's sample size, not counting the almost-marrieds, I'd say the odds are one in ten."

He grins. "There you go. Nine times out of ten I won't have to kiss you."

Have to kiss me? I'm a little miffed that he didn't like it as much as I thought he did. It seems that, even though he understood *I* wanted no-strings sex, what *he* wants is just a trip to Vegas. I must've been imagining that husky tone. How could I have been so wrong? Thank God I didn't just strip naked to get my message across. He'd probably hand me my clothes and tell me to get dressed again.

"Does that make mathematical sense?" he asks.

"Yes, of course."

"Glad we got that settled. So, ready for dinner and a show in an hour?"

I roll onto my back. "I'm still on sensory overload."

He stands and stretches. "I take it you're an introvert."

I prop up on my elbows to look at him. "And you're an extrovert."

"It helps when you're the mayor to gain energy the more people you talk to. I'm nearly always in a crowd. How about we mix it up? We'll do an introvert thing tonight for you, and tomorrow we'll do dinner and a show."

How would he know what an introvert thing is? I see now we wouldn't be compatible. We're complete opposites—extrovert and introvert. And he doesn't think fighting is a big deal. I value peace and quiet too much to be tangled up in emotional arguments with a man. I had enough of that with my sister and my mom butting heads growing up. It got loud in our tiny apartment.

"Well?" he asks.

"What kind of introvert thing?"

"When in Venice…"

"Isn't it when in Rome?"

"Go with me on this one."

Levi

Galena lets out a soft sigh as we float in a gondola on a canal inside the huge resort. The long, black flat-bottomed boat is more comfortable than I thought it would be. We're on a red leather cushioned seat facing the gondolier, a young woman in a blue and white striped shirt with a red scarf around her neck, a red sash belt, and a straw hat. Looks authentic to me.

So I didn't expect a trip to Vegas to mean everything, but I thought it was the start of *something*. Galena just wants sex. Not saying I'm turning down sex, but I'd hoped for sex plus something more. I like her a lot, and I was glad to finally get my chance with her after two months of seeing her around town and wishing she weren't with the guy who didn't deserve her.

I'm trying not to let my optimistic expectations ruin our time together. Who knows, maybe after a week together, she'll feel differently. As long as it's something real, and I'm not just the rebound guy. That would be the worst.

"It's peaceful, isn't it?" I ask.

Galena nods, a serene smile on her beautiful face. My heart beats faster, my gut tightening with desire. This woman does something to me with just a smile.

We float past a replica of St. Mark's Square, as the sign says. There's a bridge up ahead and to my left a plaza with shops and restaurants. They even have old-fashioned street-lamps made of wrought iron, each one aglow with multiple lights.

And then the gondolier surprises us by singing in Italian!

Galena's eyes are wide as she looks at me with a huge smile.

I can't resist giving her hand a squeeze. "I've always wanted to go to Italy," I whisper.

"It never crossed my mind until now," she whispers back.

After three songs, we return to a comfortable silence.

"This is so cool," Galena whispers. "I can only imagine how the real thing would be. Magical."

I keep my voice low, leaning close to her ear. "We can get dinner at one of the Italian restaurants here. I'll ask for a table in the back for quiet."

"How are you so good at the introvert thing?"

I laugh. "Mom and my sister are introverts. True book-worms. Dad and I were always the more outgoing ones. It all balances out."

We get out of the gondola near a restaurant the gondolier recommends. It's not yet prime dinnertime, so I don't think it'll be a problem getting a table.

The Italian restaurant has frescoes on the walls done in golden tones with several tables out front, along with a more private back room. White tablecloths, cloth napkins, crystal glasses. The gondolier chose well. There are a few couples here, not too crowded yet. I go to the front desk to request a quiet table in the back room.

"Let me check on that," he says.

Galena smooths her floral dress down and stares at her sneakers. "Do you think I should've changed? I'm not sure if I'm dressed for this place."

"It's Vegas. They're used to people coming in all kinds of outfits straight from the casino. They're not going to kick us out. I'm wearing shorts."

"But you're wearing cute leather boat shoes. I'm wearing sneakers."

"Your dress is fantastic."

She laughs. "Fantastic, huh?"

"All those buttons and roses. Really catches the eye."

She does a double take, checking if I'm joking. It's a little embarrassing how much I've thought of those buttons. And unbuttoning them, one by one, inch by inch.

"Thanks," she says warmly, deciding I'm being sincere. "You make khaki shorts look good. And crisp cotton T-shirts too. Really catches the eye." She stares at my shoul-der, her gaze shifting to my chest. I work out, and I'm glad to see she appreciates that. You know what? Sex is a great start.

I drop my voice to a husky register. "Thank you."

Her cheeks flush, and she looks away shyly. It must've taken a lot of nerve for her to tell me she wanted to explore her wild side with me. She seems a bit shy about sexy stuff.

The host returns with menus. "We haven't opened the back room yet, but it's ready now. You'll be the first to be seated there."

"Great, thanks so much," I say.

I put a hand on Galena's back, guiding her in with me. She flushes and glances up at me.

"Are you here for business or pleasure," the host asks us as we walk to the back room. He's a young guy with short red hair.

"Pleasure," Galena says. "My business is far from here."

She's adorably factual about everything. Earlier she told me the exact square footage of our hotel room. I looked it up, and she was right.

"We're newlyweds," I lie.

Galena's brows shoot up as she gives me a pointed look.

"Wonderful," the host says. "Congratulations!" He helps Galena with her chair and hands her a menu.

I take a seat, and he hands me a menu too.

"Would you like some complimentary champagne?" he asks us.

"We'd love some," I say.

As soon as he leaves, Galena whispers fiercely, "We can't lie!"

"No one's going to check. Newlyweds get perks. You're not obligated to do anything other than enjoy champagne, get some extra-special treatment, and maybe a free dessert. You deserve it. This is your honeymoon, after all."

She takes off her glasses and cleans them with a cloth napkin. "Don't remind me."

"Sorry. I hope your experience will be far superior with me."

She blinks at me a few times before putting her glasses back on. "How would you feel about sitting by the pool and reading a book tomorrow?"

"Sounds like a good way to spend an afternoon. I heard they have cabanas with bar service and food delivery from a gourmet restaurant."

She smiles, a soft look in her eyes. "You're so agreeable. I thought at first we'd argue over what to do, but you seem happy to do what I want."

"We're still doing dinner and a show tomorrow, which I wanted."

She nods once. "It's only fair to take turns doing what each of us likes."

"What do you think we'd fight about if we had a fight?"

She cocks her head. "I have no idea. You seem like a world-class negotiator. Seems like all that time as mayor has really helped you. Have you had a lot of successful relationships?"

I'm surprised she's asking. Is she considering me as a potential relationship candidate? I'm getting really mixed signals here. Maybe part of her wants to be with me, but she's just not ready right now. That's understandable since she was just left at the altar yesterday. It *has* been a whirlwind.

On the other hand, my experience is not so great, and I hate to say it because it makes me sound like I'm not capable of commitment when I'm sure I could be with the right woman. I thought Alissa was that woman for a while. I want someone to share my life with.

"Let me make it easy on you," she says. "Just answer yes or no to having a lot of successful relationships."

"No."

"Hmm…"

I try to come up with an explanation that makes me look good. I got bored or it just never worked out seems lame. Thankfully, she jumps in.

"Kevin was my one and only serious relationship. You know how that went."

It hits me that she brought up relationships to let me know she's only been with one guy. I choose my words carefully.

"So did you date before him, but it never went anywhere?"

"Let's see." She looks to the ceiling and back to me. "Two years and two months with Kevin was my longest relationship, and it was smooth sailing all the way to the end. Guess you couldn't call that a success anymore. In grad school, I was with another stats student for a month. Before that, nothing lasted for more than two dates. I just lost interest, or they did." That last part was mumbled.

"Would it sound bad to say I've never had anything last past a month?"

"Would it sound bad to say I've only ever been with one guy?"

"By been with, do you mean…"

She slaps the table. "Yup."

If she's only had sex with one guy, her claim to want no-strings sex with me doesn't quite ring true. It seems she's never done that before, so why would she say that unless she considered the potential for something more? That must be it. She's nervous after her failed wedding, that's all. I relax a little. I'm not the rebound guy. I'm the guy she really wants to be with. She just has to learn she can trust me.

The waiter arrives just then with two glasses of sparkling champagne and a small plate of prosciutto-wrapped something.

"Congratulations," the waiter says as he sets everything down. "These are prosciutto-wrapped figs compliments of the chef."

"Thank you," I say.

"Thanks," Galena echoes, looking guilty about our complimentary honeymoon gifts.

As soon as the waiter leaves, I tell her, "Relax. They're set up for this. I'm sure they have tons of champagne and figs for all the newlyweds who come here." I hold up my glass to toast her.

She holds up her glass. "I don't like to lie. First we let my grandparents think you were my husband, and now we're fake honeymooners at a restaurant. This is out of control."

"To out-of-control fun," I say, clinking her glass with mine. I take a sip of champagne. It's good.

She exhales sharply. "I did promise myself I'd have more fun and not think so much about the odds of success." She takes a cautious sip of champagne. "Mmm, that's really good." She takes another sip and then tries one of the figs.

I try one too. The salty prosciutto goes well with the sweet fig.

By the time we finish our champagne, Galena is noticeably more relaxed. She sighs and leans back in her chair. "Now that I'm at the table, no one can see my sneakers, so I fit in better. Ahhh. This is the life."

"Agreed."

The waiter returns to take our order. I order a steak Florentine, and Galena goes for the chicken fricassee.

She leans toward me across the table. "Sooo, are you a commitment-phobe? Just curious."

I sit up straighter. She's definitely considering me as a potential relationship candidate. "I'm open to a relationship with the *right* woman."

Her cheeks flush, and she smooths her hair back over her ears, looking away.

Another couple comes into the back room.

"Darn," Galena whispers.

They're seated at the table in the corner, behind us. "We're on our honeymoon," the woman says to the host.

"Wonderful! Congratulations," the host says just like he said to us. "Would you like some complimentary champagne?"

I lift my brows at Galena, who covers a laugh.

The host leaves.

Galena leans close to whisper, "You were right. And I don't see wedding bands on them either."

I lean across the table, close enough to feel that charge of electricity whenever we get close. "Not everyone wears a wedding band."

"Kiss the bride," the woman says to the man she's with. Husband? Boyfriend?

"You know what that means," I tell Galena, half joking, half not. I said I'd only kiss her if someone said to kiss the bride.

"Yes, I know," she whispers and closes her eyes.

I cup her jaw and give her a soft kiss that sends a jolt through me on contact. I pull back to check in with her, and she grabs my head, kissing me like she means business. Raw lust surges through me.

"Woohoo!" the woman at the next table calls. "Looks like we've got more newlyweds in here!"

Galena jerks away, glancing at the woman, who wiggles her fingers at her and smiles. Galena gives her a slight wave and turns back to me, whispering, "Sorry. I don't know what came over me." She stares at the table. "I'm not into public displays."

I lift her chin. "I liked it."

She looks around. "I think we need more champagne."

9

Galena

The champagne combined with the tumult of the last couple of days wipes me out. I barely have the energy to change into a tank top and sweatpants and brush my teeth before collapsing in bed. Even so, I'm conscious of Levi moving around the room until he settles into the bed next to mine. He doesn't even try to make a move. I'm a teensy bit disappointed, which is ridiculous. I'm in no shape to start anything at the moment.

Next thing I know, it's morning. It's still dim in the room, just a bit of light peeking through the curtains. I check the time on the clock on the nightstand. Five forty-five a.m. Well, I was in bed by nine. I look over at Levi. One bare muscular arm is on top of the covers as he sleeps peacefully on his side, facing me. There's just enough room for me in there. I could really use some cuddle time. Or more. This could be the easiest path to seduction. I debate stripping out of my tank top and sweatpants and quickly decide it's too forward. Let him meet me halfway.

I slip into bed with him, lying on my side, my back to his chest like two spoons, and pull his arm around my middle. It's wonderful. Like lying in a big warm teddy bear's arms. I really like Levi. He makes me feel safe and excited at the same time. I didn't know that was possible. My entire body relaxes against his heat. It's been so long since I've been held. Kevin was late to bed, and I was early to rise. Not that he was ever much of a cuddler.

I don't want to think about the past, or worry about the future. I just want to enjoy this moment wrapped in a cocoon of delicious heat.

Not that Levi is enjoying this too. I'm making him cuddle me. I feel too good to be guilty over that. His warm brown eyes come to mind, the crinkles at the corners of his eyes when he smiles. I bet if he were awake and I asked him to cuddle me, he'd open the covers and say, "Sure, why not?" My eyes drift closed.

I wake to a bright room. Crap. I didn't mean to fall asleep. Something hard pokes into my hip, and an excited tingle rushes through me. Does he desire me? He didn't exactly say he was on board with a sexcapade when I mentioned it. It could be morning wood. Kevin told me it doesn't mean a guy is interested; it's just a biological thing that happens while he sleeps. Very common.

I peek over my shoulder.

He's still sleeping. That was just biology poking into my hip. Damn. I shouldn't even be here cuddling an unsuspecting man.

I slip out of bed, feeling horribly guilty. That's the last time, I swear.

Levi

Galena cuddled up against me this morning. I don't know how long she was there. I woke up having a dream that I held her in my arms, and there she was. She smells sweet, a light fruit scent maybe from her shampoo; her skin is so soft, her curvy body fitting perfectly against mine. I wonder if she'll visit my bed again tomorrow. I hope so. I considered making a move and decided it was too soon. I want her to know she can trust me with more than her body. I'm not going to be the rebound guy again.

Room service arrives, and I let them in. I ordered us breakfast. Galena is still in the bathroom getting ready.

I tip the guy and settle into our sunken living room in a T-shirt and shorts, adding cream to my coffee. I take a fortifying sip. I'll leave the food for when she can join me.

A few minutes later, she steps out of the steamy bathroom fully dressed in a white cover-up open in front and a full-coverage swimsuit. It's a blue short-sleeved swim shirt with a matching miniskirt. At least it clings to her sexy body. She's either modest or careful about the sun. Her hair is wet and piled on top of her head in a loose bun, glasses on, her cheeks flushed from the heat of the shower.

"Morning," I say.

"Hi!" she says in a high pitch. "How did you sleep?"

"Great. How about you?"

"Lots of sleep. Ooh, I thought I heard the door. I love room service."

"I thought you might. An introvert's dream."

She laughs as she approaches. "It's nice you understand our kind." She sits next to me on the sofa and lifts the dome over a breakfast plate. "I love French toast! But what are you going to eat?"

I nudge her arm. "We can't share?"

"Oh. Yeah. Of course." She sounds incredibly disappointed.

"Kidding. I'm good with the fruit."

She glances at my small fruit salad before diving into the French toast. There's whipped cream and strawberry slices on top. She chews with her eyes closed, her face lifted in pure pleasure. Desire coils low in my belly.

She takes a drink of water. "It's weird, but I feel like we already know each other so well."

"Full confession. Your grandmother told me you loved French toast. We talked quite a bit about you while we played slots together. This was after you dashed off for more mathematically reasonable pastures."

She takes another forkful of French toast. "They love you already. No wonder you're such a popular mayor."

"How do you know I'm popular?"

"Kayla told me everyone loves you. She secretly thought you should go for her friend Audrey, who apparently has a monster crush on some guy who's not interested at all. But Audrey only sees you as a friend because you grew up together."

"Yeah, well, that's what happens when you live in your hometown. Lots of women I've known since elementary school."

A smile plays over her lips. "Not me."

I fight the urge to kiss her. "Not you."

I take the covering off my fruit salad and eat my breakfast while she finishes hers.

As soon as she's done, she flops back on the sofa. "I'm having a great time on our vacation, and I wasn't expecting…" She trails off and studies me. "Are you having a good time?"

"I am. I got us tickets for the cirque show tonight and made reservations for dinner nearby."

"Don't forget reading by the pool. I'm already in my swimsuit."

I take a closer look. "I've never seen a swimsuit like that. It's almost like a dress."

"Skin cancer."

"You've had it?"

"No, I don't want to get it. The stats on it are scary. This is a super SPF cover-up swim shirt over the swimsuit. I'll also be wearing sunscreen, polarized sunglasses, and a floppy hat."

"Won't you be hot?"

"Actually, I'm hot right now. I can always take a dip in the pool to cool off." She stands and takes off her cover-up.

I sip my coffee, pretending not to notice as she then peels

off her swim shirt. The swimsuit underneath is tank style, not terribly revealing skin-wise, but it emphasizes her curves in a way that has every part of me standing at attention.

I set my coffee down. "I'm going to take a shower." I stride to the bathroom before she can notice how much I want her.

"But you didn't finish your breakfast!" she calls. "It's the most important meal of the day."

I stick my head out of the bathroom. "I'm leaving room for our fantastic dinner tonight."

Her eyes light up. "Ooh!"

I love that she's into food. Some of the women I've dated have been on diets that made them cranky, and God forbid if I ate stuff in front of them they felt they shouldn't have.

Once I'm in the shower, I give my throbbing erection some much-needed relief. Thoughts of Galena flood my brain, her body curved against mine this morning, the pleasure on her face while she ate breakfast, those luscious lips. The lower lip fuller than the top. Oh God.

There's a knock at the door.

I still, on the brink. "Just a minute!"

"I have a confession," she says through the door.

I'm intrigued, but there's some urgency here, and if she opens that door, she's going to see me through the glass shower door, fully erect and ready to burst. "Can it wait a few minutes?"

The door opens. "What?"

"I said…never mind."

I turn off the water, grab a towel, and wrap it around myself.

"Don't worry, I'll keep my eyes closed," she says.

I wipe some condensation from the glass to see her more clearly. She's wearing her glasses, eyes closed tight. "I stole a cuddle from you while you were sleeping. The guilt is killing me. Sorry I did that without asking."

I debate the right thing to say here. Should I say she can climb into my bed whenever she wants, or should I just say no problem? I want to encourage bed sharing without scaring her off.

She steps closer. "Did you hear what I said?"

"You felt so guilty you had to interrupt my shower?"

Her eyes open, her lips parting as she sees me through the glass door, still dripping wet. "Sorry!" She closes her eyes again. "Double sorry. It was the guilt. Oh man, I made it worse." She turns and bumps into the sink counter. "Ow!" She must've opened her eyes after that because she makes it to the door without any further injury.

I'm torn between a laugh and wanting to drag her sexy self into the shower with me. I set the towel back on the hook and start the water again. I didn't get a chance to wash yet. After that, I've got to make a move on her. This is torture.

She stops in the doorway and speaks to the ceiling. "Do you forgive me?"

"Yes."

She mumbles something I can't make out and finally leaves. I wash up, thinking of her guilt and need to confess all. Then I think about how open she's been with me. She admitted to a lackluster sex life with her ex, told me he was the only guy she'd been with, and confirmed she wanted a week of no-strings sex with me. Two things become crystal clear in that moment—Galena is a woman who's direct and honest. And she wants me bad. What am I waiting for? Sex can be a good start to a relationship, I assure myself. No need to go excruciatingly slow.

A man can only take so much.

I quickly finish in the shower and step back in the room, a towel wrapped around my waist. She's standing at the large window, looking out at the view of Vegas. There's something different about her. Ah, she took off her glasses.

I join her there, and she meets my eyes briefly and then stares at my chest and then lower, down to my abs and the towel hung loosely around my hips. "Nice view," I say.

"Yes," she says in a breathy voice.

My lips curve up. She means me. "No glasses today?"

"I figured I'd wear my prescription sunglasses at the pool. I'm nearsighted."

"So you can see me clearly, then."

"Very much." She sounds happy about that.

I'm dying to touch her but refrain. She has to make the first move so I know she's ready. She did just end an engagement a few days ago.

"Levi?"

"Yeah?" My voice sounds husky.

"When I cuddled you, it seemed like maybe you—" she holds up a palm "—no, never mind. Biology."

"Biology?"

She exhales sharply and gives me a matter-of-fact look. "I know about morning wood."

I bite back a smile. "Do you know what it does to a guy to feel a sexy woman pressed against him?"

Her eyes widen. "You think I'm sexy? Wait, you were awake?"

"Yes to both. I woke up just a few minutes before you left the bed."

She touches her forehead. "And I was so guilty I barged in on your shower to confess."

"I liked having you in bed with me."

Her eyes light up. "I loved being there. It was wonderful. You're wonderful."

She thinks I'm wonderful. That means she's seeing this as more than just a casual thing.

She lifts a hand toward my shoulder, and I go stock-still, letting her make her move.

She drops her hand abruptly. "We can't tell my grandparents we're in the honeymoon suite together. We'll probably see them again this week, so it would be best if we said we were in separate rooms."

"Okay by me."

She stares straight ahead. "My family thinks I'm a little too free with guys, though I've only been with one guy."

"If you've only been with one guy, why does your family think you're too free with guys?"

"No sex before marriage. They weren't happy with me when I moved in with Kevin. They pretended he didn't exist. In fact, they never wanted to meet him, which is why my grandparents assumed you were him since they hadn't met him before. Anyway, they were finally okay with it when I said we were going to make it official."

"Okay," I say slowly. I can only imagine how hard it is to live by her family's standards. She's racked with guilt way too much. Though I suppose it's good to know she always wants to be honest. It sounds like she's still on the fence about getting physical with me, purely from a guilt perspective.

I think about our options. "So we're either married and having approved sex, or not married and not having any sex. Which do you prefer?"

She stares at my mouth and licks her lips. Does she know what she does to me?

I inch closer. "Galena?"

"I don't like either of those options, but I really like the way you say 'sex.'"

Every part of me rises to attention. Who knew honesty could be so sexy? Her gaze locks on mine, and the blood rushes through my veins.

I close the curtains in one quick jerk.

"Kiss the bride," she says.

I don't need any more encouragement than that. She made the first move. I curl my hand at the back of her neck, pull her close, and kiss her.

Galena

I don't know what's come over me. One minute I get a clueless text from Kevin asking where I am, and the next moment Levi's up close in only a towel, and I'm kissing him like a wild woman.

My hands take on a life of their own, roaming and squeezing all that hard hot muscle. Passion sweeps me away. I'm dizzy with lust. Crazy hot.

He breaks the kiss, nuzzling into my neck, sending electric tingles through me everywhere he touches. I'm aching and dying to get closer. I yank off his towel. His gaze meets mine, smoldering hot.

I glance down at a magnificent erection. I did that. He's the sexiest man I've ever seen, and he wants me. I struggle to get my swimsuit off; the thing's clinging to me. It's new for my trip, and the material is unforgivingly tight. "Get this off me!"

Levi pushes my hands away and peels it off me easily. Cool air meets hot skin, and I sigh. No time to be self-conscious with this newly discovered passion. I wrap my arms around his neck, plastering my body against his as I kiss him hungrily, our tongues tangling.

He backs me up and then lifts me. I wrap my arms and legs around him as he carries me up the two stairs to the bedroom.

He sets me gently on his bed, the blanket still pushed to the side, and I land on the cool sheet. He covers me with his body, kissing me deeply. The unusual scrape of his beard against me, his fresh clean scent, the heat of his hard body. All of it combines in a cloud of sensation.

I break the kiss, gasping for air. "I want you so bad."

He nips my lower lip and then sucks. "I love your honesty."

"Okay. So there's a condom in my bag."

"Mine too. Looks like we're both prepared for any eventuality."

"I love that you're prepared. Responsibility is sexy."

He chuckles low and then kisses along my collarbone, his hands caressing my breasts. Oh my. I've never felt that before. His thumbs brush back and forth across my nipples, and ripples of sensation wash through my body.

"Oh my God," I say. "That feels so good."

He stills and meets my eyes. "Is this new for you?"

"Yes."

"Did you save yourself for marriage, even though you lived with your ex?"

My face flushes. "No, but, uh, I've only been with Kevin, and he was kinda efficient. Just the important parts. You know what I mean?"

"There are a lot of important parts."

Before I can explain what I mean, his mouth closes over my nipple and sucks. A tension low in my belly and then a throbbing even lower shock me. My fingers slide into his hair, keeping him there, awash with pleasure.

He switches sides, his hand roaming down my body, sliding along my inner thigh. My breath hitches in anticipation, my hips rising to meet him.

"I need…oh God, I need."

He lifts his head. "Need is good. Stay with that for a while."

A while?

And then he kisses a straight line down to my throbbing center, and I cry out, the pleasure so intense I can barely comprehend it. And then his big hands spread me farther, settling my legs over his shoulders.

I take one look at him between my legs and let out a long low moan I didn't know I was capable of. Pleasure crashes over me in wave after wave, higher and higher, my insides coiling tighter. I've never felt so much, too much. I tug on his hair, pulling him away.

He looks up at me in question.

"It's a little intense for me. I'm not used to—"

He dives back in, and I'm right back on the sharp edge of pleasure, writhing under him until he holds me still. Primal sounds emerge from my throat, my body bows off the bed, and then I break as the orgasm slams into me, shaking me to my core. I rock helplessly under him as he draws out every last drop of pleasure until I go limp.

He kisses his way up my body. "I like being your first for some things."

"That was my first orgasm with a guy."

He closes his eyes, looking pained. I want to tell him it's okay because I know how to make myself feel good, but the intensity of what he brought me is ten times what my own efforts produce. It's not okay that I was ready to settle for less. I see that now.

A rush of affection has me hugging him tight. "Thank you. You're wonderful." I kiss him. "Amazing. I'm so lucky. Oh, you taste like…me, I guess."

He cradles my jaw. "You're so sexy, so sweet. I'm the lucky one."

I wrap my legs high around his waist in response.

He gazes deep into my eyes, and then finally we join. Raw pleasure rockets through me with every thrust. I rock my hips, and he moves faster and faster, driving me to higher levels of pleasure. And then he hits just the right angle. A deep orgasm rocks me, sensation radiating out in a starburst through my body.

He groans, pleasure washing over his handsome face as he finally lets himself go, holding me tight to him. Every movement brings more pleasure. Finally, he stills.

I blink a few times as something occurs to me. "We forgot the condom, didn't we?"

He mutters a curse.

"Don't worry, I'm on the pill. Since my ex didn't want kids, we used double protection. Pills and condom."

"Good." He lifts his head. "Could we maybe not talk about your ex while we're naked?"

I pat his shoulder. "Of course. There's no comparison, honestly. I—"

He kisses me, cutting me off. I lose myself in the kiss, drenched in pleasure and so deeply content. When he finally lets me up for air, he says, "I'm going to marry you one day."

I beam because I know what he really means. "That's the

sex talking. You must've really liked it. I did too, if you couldn't tell."

He brushes his thumb over my lower lip. "I could tell, and that's not the sex talking, it's me."

I push at his chest, panicking. He's thinking of marriage? I just broke up with someone I nearly married! "It's too soon!"

He cups my jaw, his warm eyes like a caress. His voice is silky smooth. "Don't worry. And no guilt. Only pleasure." And then he kisses me again, and my mind shuts down. How can I argue when it feels so right?

10

———————

Levi

This whole week has been a blur. Today's our last day of vacation, and we're driving with Galena's grandparents in the back seat to the Grand Canyon. Galena's driving, so I can relax. We explored all Las Vegas has to offer with introvert breaks by the pool and occasional room service. Besides the cirque show, we went to a bunch of casinos, a comedy show, a concert, rode a huge Ferris wheel, and went to the pinball hall of fame. I own a vintage pinball machine, so I had to check it out. Galena got really into it too.

I haven't pushed her for more than she's able to give, coming fresh off a breakup, but she climbs into my bed every night. I'm going to marry this woman one day. I said it in the heat of the moment, but I meant it. I don't know if it's her refreshing honesty, her sharply inquisitive mind, or her sexy good looks. Probably all of the above and more. She gets my sense of humor. We laugh a lot.

I lean my head back on the headrest and close my eyes. Only problem is, she's going back to a house that includes her ex. He's been texting and calling her every day. Not cool. She hasn't returned his calls as far as I know, though she did text back to say she's visiting her grandparents. She didn't want him to call out a search party for a missing person.

I told her to block his number, but she won't. To me that's a red flag that things aren't completely over with him. I can't let myself think about that. Otherwise, this whole awesome experience is tainted.

"You awake up there?" Betsy asks from the back seat, poking my shoulder. I like Galena's grandmother. For someone so traditional, she knows how to let loose.

"I'm awake."

"Thanks for making the early morning drive so we wouldn't get back too late. Mr. Torres is asleep by nine o'clock every night."

"I can stay up later if I want," Mr. Torres says indignantly.

"You tried on New Year's Eve, and you fell asleep at eight thirty in your recliner."

"That's because I had two beers. That would make any man fall asleep, right, Levi?"

Only two beers puts him to sleep? "Right."

"See, Levi knows the deal," he says. "Good to finally have another man in the family. I've been outnumbered for a long time."

"Ahem," Betsy says.

"Which I feel very fortunate about," Mr. Torres adds.

"Swedish fish?" Betsy asks, holding the bag out to me.

"Sure." I take some and offer the bag to Galena.

"I don't want to get my fingers sticky on the wheel. Can you put it in my mouth?"

My dirty mind immediately imagines her saying that in a naked situation, and every part of me heats. I bite back what I want to say, *happy to put it in your mouth, anytime,* and feed her a candy fish.

She chews happily, unaware of any sexy vibe from me. I do keep her well satisfied at night and sometimes again in the morning. The list of things she's never tried in bed is astonishingly long considering she was in a two-year relationship. Her ex kept it all about him, and the whole thing took five minutes tops. Yes, she told me all the details in her honest way. I didn't mind hearing it because every word out of her mouth only confirmed that he didn't deserve her.

I can't see any world where she'd want to go back to that kind of sex life. Still, you never know when it comes to the heart. Maybe he has something else that keeps her tethered to him. She won't cut ties, and it bugs me more than it should considering I've only been with her for a week.

"Soda?" Betsy asks. "I also have sparkling water and flavored iced tea."

"Grandmom, you didn't have to bring so much. They have restaurants at the Grand Canyon."

"You always want to have lots of food and drink when you're crossing the Mojave desert. People come unprepared, their car breaks down, and they—" she lowers her voice to the softest of whispers "—die."

"Knock wood," Mr. Torres says, knocking my head.

"Grandpop!" Galena exclaims. "Don't knock his head."

I laugh. "I'm fine."

She rubs my head with one hand, her eyes never leaving the road. "Is your family like this?"

"I'd have to say no. I'm probably the most outgoing one. Mom and Avery are more the quiet sorts. Like you."

"Galena's not quiet," Betsy says, sounding shocked. "You should hear her at home. Singing in the shower, bossing her big sister around, getting fresh with her mother."

Galena rolls her eyes.

"Rolling her eyes!" Betsy says, pointing at her. "See? The girl's got spirit. Always has."

"I like her spirit," I say.

"I grew up," Galena says. "I'm not getting fresh with anyone. Geez."

"Fresh," Betsy says.

"That was fresh," Mr. Torres says.

"Ugh!" Galena exclaims.

"Anyone want licorice?" Betsy asks.

"Did you pack anything healthy?" Galena asks. "If we keep eating junk on our four-hour drive, we're going to puke when we get there, and then how can we admire the Grand Canyon?"

"That is *rude* talk," Betsy says. "We don't say puke. It's not ladylike."

"Nope," Mr. Torres chimes in. "That's not how you were raised."

Galena's fingers tighten on the steering wheel, her mouth clamped shut. I guess this is also what she meant when she said her grandparents were traditional.

"I hope you don't speak to Levi in such a crass way," Betsy says.

"I'm fine," I say.

"There's still appropriate and inappropriate," Betsy says.

"I love inappropriate," I say, and Galena bursts out laughing.

My chest puffs with pride. No question we belong together. I know how to make her laugh, how to make her feel good, and I think I could make her happy. Long term. I just have to get her ex out of the picture.

Galena

After an excruciating four-hour drive with my grandparents—I forgot how close quarters can make things tense between us—we're out in the wide-open spaces of the Grand Canyon. It's a comfortable eighty degrees, unlike Vegas, which hit a hundred and four degrees yesterday.

We take the South Rim trail, which is supposed to be easy. Paved and flat with views of the Grand Canyon and the Colorado River. My grandparents are walking several paces behind us, holding hands. It's weird, but I don't feel right holding Levi's hand in public, even though we're together every night. That part is like our private cocoon in the dark. I admit I've still got my ex on my mind. It's hard to completely move on after more than two years. He's been sending increasingly heartfelt apologies each day as he misses me more and more. He doesn't know I'm here with Levi, because I only told him I was visiting my grandparents. A lie of omission. The guilt is killing me, even though part of me says Kevin shouldn't matter anymore. He walked out on our wedding.

I wish this vacation could go on forever. I know everything will change when I get back home, dealing with my ex and all my hurt feelings over our failed wedding, getting my house back and Kevin out of it. I just really needed a break, where I didn't have to think about any of that. And where does Levi fit in my real life? I'm just not sure I can risk my heart again. I fear I've already let myself feel too much.

Levi and I stop at a lookout and take in the view in a corner spot by the railing away from the tourists.

"Let me get your picture," Grandpop says.

We turn to face him, and Levi puts his arm around me. I flush with heat, and then I'm instantly embarrassed that my lust is showing. My grandparents think Levi is the whirlwind romance that they had, with a proper courtship and wedding bells in our future.

Grandmom beams at us.

"Galena, smile!" Grandpop orders.

"I am smiling," I say through my teeth.

"A real smile," he says.

Levi looks at me with concern, and my eyes get hot. He kisses my temple. "It's okay. We don't have to."

"No, take the picture." I force my mind to Levi and me at the concert last night, watching an Elvis impersonator, sharing a popcorn, and then dancing in our seats. A wonderfully carefree happy time. I have to stop worrying about the future. Tomorrow is soon enough to be slammed into real life.

"There she is," Grandpop says, taking our picture.

"Levi, take our picture," Grandmom says.

We switch places, and Levi snaps a bunch of pictures of my grandparents and then some with me too.

As soon as we move to the next part of the trail, Grandmom walks with me. "Something on your mind?"

I glance at Levi. He gives me a subtle nod and hangs back to join Grandpop, who stopped to read a trail sign.

"No," I lie. So much is on my mind about going back home and picking up the pieces of my life I don't know where to start.

She gives me a hug. "I know something's bothering you. It must be a difficult time for you, though I can see Levi is a bright spot."

We walk down the path together. "Everything I thought made sense about the world no longer applies. Like with Kevin."

"What do you mean?"

"We had similar schedules, both of us dedicated to our work. And we never had a single argument. It seemed like the next logical step to get married after we bought a house together. I was so wrong."

She puts her arm around me and gives me a squeeze. "Oh, Galena. The heart doesn't care about logic. I'm glad it ended if that was the kind of love you had. Your sister could never put her finger on why she didn't like him. Maybe she saw that it wasn't true love between you two."

"Izzy did say he's selfish."

"Is he?"

I think back to how he wanted me to cater to his needs on the same day he left me at the altar, how he never took care of me when I was sick, even though I always took care of him, the way he was selfish in bed, which I didn't know until Levi. I was so inexperienced I thought it was normal. It's a little embarrassing to admit my first orgasm with a partner was with Levi. Kevin would ask me if I was okay afterward, and I always said yes. Why didn't I ask for more? I was just content that it was over, and now I could move on to the next thing on my to-do list.

That sounds awful in hindsight.

I press my lips together. "Yes, Kevin is very selfish."

"It's hard to love someone who doesn't give back."

"I thought I loved him, but now I'm questioning everything."

She smiles. "Because of Levi."

"I'm so confused right now."

"You're happy when you're with Levi. It's written all over your face, and you laugh together. That makes for the best of marriages. Like me and Grandpop."

"Oh, we're not getting married."

She pats my arm. "I hope for a truly giddy kind of happiness for you in your next relationship. When you can't wait to see him and you miss him when you're apart. I want you to have a love of the soul not just the mind or the body."

My face flushes. I suppose Kevin and I were an affair of the mind. With Levi, I'm feeling much more of the body. I hope it doesn't show since my grandparents wouldn't approve.

"I really like Levi," Grandmom says.

"I do too," I admit.

I glance over at Levi and Grandpop in deep conversation. Levi looks awfully serious. What're they talking about?

"Of course, you're the one who has to be brave enough to open your heart again," Grandmom says. "Take your time but not too long. I imagine Levi is well liked by everyone, including single women."

At my dark look, she arches her brows.

"Come on, there's more to see," I call to Levi and Grandpop.

Levi's eye catches mine. Something's up. I hope Grandpop didn't say the wrong thing.

~

Levi

I catch up to Galena and take her hand. She pulls her hand from mine, and my gut turns over. It's like her grandfather said, she's not ready for me.

"I feel weird touching in front of them," she says.

My gut churns. "Your grandfather says you never rush into things." *And that I'm a rebound to help you get over Kevin.*

It's more than that, isn't it?

My gut says *no* as it churns on.

"That's true," she says. "I always look at a situation from every angle and calculate the odds of success. I don't want to be that person anymore. I want to follow my instincts. I just have to find those instincts. I'm sort of out of practice with listening to my gut."

A small sliver of hope slides through just as a breeze picks up, tossing her long hair into her face. I smooth her hair back from her face, and then I can't resist stroking her round cheek.

Her lips part as she gazes into my eyes. "Hi."

I smile. "Hi."

It's like a new beginning, a real one for the two of us. She's willing to follow her instincts, and that means I have a chance. We're good together. I want to kiss her so bad, but her grandparents are right behind us.

"Who's hungry?" Betsy asks. "I could go for some lunch."

Galena laughs as her grandparents join us. "Didn't you fill up on Swedish fish and licorice?"

"Oh, I never eat candy. That's just for you kids."

Galena shoots me an amused look. "She thinks we're kids."

"And I thought thirty was the end," I say, only half kidding. Some part of me believes I won't make it past Dad's age. Like father like son in so many ways.

"Ha!" Mr. Torres says. "Thirty is still young. You haven't hit your prime yet."

"When's that?" They look to be in their seventies.

"Fifty," he says with confidence.

"I think sixty," Betsy says.

"Seventy for you, my love," Mr. Torres says. "You've never looked more beautiful."

She rubs his chest. "Nick."

"The older you get, the more you think the needle moves on old age," Galena says. "When you're eighty, you'll think ninety isn't that old after all. It's all a matter of perception."

Betsy throws her arms around Galena. "You'll always be my bossy little Lena."

"Lena?" I ask.

"Childhood nickname," Galena says. "I go by my full name now because I like the meaning. It's an old Greek name that means tranquil. Mom picked it from a baby name book, hoping I'd be a calm baby after my energetic sister. Anyway, that's how I like my life to be."

"Then what're you doing in Las Vegas?" Betsy asks. "This city likes to shake things up."

And what're you doing with me? Life as the mayor of Summerdale is anything but tranquil. I'm constantly putting out fires, finagling budgets with many stakeholders, showing up to every frigging event in town. It's nonstop.

They start talking about where to go for lunch, but all I hear in my mind is what her grandfather said to me earlier, "Sorry to say, you're a rebound to help her get over Kevin."

How can I be more than just the rebound guy?

11

Galena

It's our last night in Vegas, and I figure we should make the most of it. After I drop my grandparents off, I drive back to our hotel. Levi's been kinda quiet.

I glance over at him. "It's only six. The rest of the night is ours."

"Yeah. What do you want to do?"

"Everything."

"That's a long list." I can hear the smile in his voice. He's up for anything.

"There's a roller coaster at the New York-New York hotel with cute taxicab cars."

"You said you never go on coasters with loops."

I smile. "Galena 2.0 is open to new experiences. I want to try it even though I'm scared."

"Feel the fear and do it anyway, huh?"

I think about that. "Yeah, that works. Though I don't want to spend the whole night doing things that scare me. Just one thing."

"Galena, when we get back home—"

"No talking about home. Just focus on the moment. Please, Levi, I want to have fun."

He's quiet.

"Okay?" I prompt.

"Okay. Tonight's all about fun. I can look up some cool things to do we haven't tried yet."

"Yes!"

"Good thing we dropped off your grandparents, or we'd be tied to the slots and then straight to bed."

"No, you'd be tied to the slots with Grandmom, and I'd be at the poker table with Grandpop."

He drums his fingers on the dashboard. "They're good people. And still so into each other."

"Yeah. They're coming up on their fifty-fifth anniversary soon."

"Wow."

"My eyes are open now, Levi. I didn't have that kind of relationship before, and I want that."

"Me too."

I glance over at him, suddenly nervous. Are we jumping into the deep end of a committed relationship so soon? One week after my breakup?

I clear my throat. "Not now; one day. Down the road."

"Sure." He sounds casual, but I hear a hint of sadness.

"Anyway…" I look out at the scenery as we come up on the Strip. "Here it is. Oh, look! There's the Statue of Liberty at New York-New York. Good thing we didn't eat dinner yet. Let's do that first."

"I'm game. I've got a cool lounge in mind to end the evening, real low key, and they have a live band."

"Awesome. And let's do one of those all-you-can-eat buffets too."

"You'd never get your money's worth. You only eat ninety percent of your food."

"I told you that's when I get full."

His lips curve up, his eyes sparkling in that way I'm starting to love. "There's so many interesting quirks I need to get to know about you, Galena Torres."

"I'm not quirky."

"Oh, no. Not at all, *Miss sit by the pool under an umbrella with a big floppy hat and a full coverall.*"

I laugh. "I'm protecting my skin."

"Why sit by the pool at all if you're completely covered?"

"Because it's relaxing."

"And then you're hot with the coverall, swim shirt, and swimsuit."

I bite back a laugh. "Which is why I have my two-part swimsuit system for when I want to cool off in the pool."

"But you don't get your hair wet."

"Trust me, it's not worth the effort of untangling it after chlorine and sun."

"I stand corrected. You're not quirky, you're just delightfully sensible."

I grin. "You really get me."

"I do," he says with so much husky warmth my entire body heats. And that reminds me of how much he knows in bed. The man seems to anticipate my needs, my desires, knowing just how to get me to the brink and hold me there until I finally explode. It's been phenomenal, and I suddenly want more. Like right away.

"Levi?"

"Yes, Galena?" He sounds knowing. A shiver of anticipation races down my spine.

"Can we stop in our room first?"

His hand slides to my inner thigh. "I'd love to."

Levi

I can't keep my hands off her. As soon as she parked in the garage, I lunged for her. I managed to get us out of the car, and now we're in the elevator. I swear if there weren't another couple in here, I'd have her right here against the wall.

She peeks up at me under her lashes as we stand behind the couple. I take her hand and give it a squeeze. She doesn't pull away. It about killed me when she pulled away before.

It's probably lust keeping her close to me, but I'll work with what I have.

We get to the lobby and take another elevator to our room. The moment the doors open on our floor, I grab her hand and practically run to our room.

"Slow down!" she says on a laugh. "I'm not going anywhere."

I unlock the door, push it open and pull her inside, kissing her and wrapping my arms around her. The door slams shut behind us. Her fingers tangle in my hair, soft sounds emanating from deep in her throat.

I turn and pin her against the door, lifting her shirt, sliding my hands over her silky soft skin. Her tongue tangles with mine. I've only caressed her breasts for a moment when she breaks the kiss and yanks my shirt off.

"God, I want you so bad," she says. "It's been so long."

My lips curve up. "Just since last night."

I yank her shorts down, dragging her panties along with them, and then I drop to my knees to kiss her where no man has ever kissed her before except *me*. Within minutes she's rocking against me, moaning loudly, and I can't help but think, *Mine*. No one else gets this. *Mine, mine, mine.*

She tastes so good, so sweet. I thrust my fingers inside her, moving in the way I know sets her off as I keep up the rhythm, loving every soft gasp out of her mouth. Moments later, she grabs my head, her fingers tightening in my hair. Her breath hitches, and then her hips jerk as she goes off, her soft cries only spurring me on. She rocks against me twice more before going utterly limp, lying back against the door.

I strip as she watches with half-hooded eyes. So sexy. I cradle her face with both hands, so much emotion flooding me in that moment I nearly admit everything I'm feeling. That she's mine. That I'm half in love with her. That I want her to be with me and only me.

"Levi, fuck me," she says, stroking me and making my eyes roll back in my head.

I lift her and thrust inside her in one swift stroke. She gasps.

I press my forehead to hers. "Hang on tight."

She wraps her arms and legs around me. "We've never done it standing up before."

"I couldn't wait. Do you want the bed?"

"No. I just want you."

Lust and raw emotion surge through me at the same time. I thrust into her over and over, taking her to the hilt. Her nails dig into my shoulders as she makes the sexiest little sounds.

"Oh my God," she says. "This feels so-ooo good."

I kiss along her neck and slip my fingers between us, stroking her as I pump slowly into her. She pants, her eyes wide open, locked on mine.

"Levi, I'm going to…I can't. Oh God."

"You can."

She's learning to ride the wave of orgasm. With me. I showed her what her body could do. *Mine, mine, mine.*

She pushes at my shoulders. "It's too much."

I kiss along her neck and then bite the cord of her neck.

She grips my shoulders tightly. "I'm too…Ahh!"

I watch as she gasps and moans and then trembles. I lean close to her ear. "Let go. Come for me."

She bucks wildly and then shouts my name. *My name.* Fierce pride bursts through my chest. I pound into her, need clawing at me as she crests wave after wave, moaning loudly with each one.

The orgasm hits hard, intense ecstasy melting my bones. I collapse against her.

She clings to me as we catch our breath.

I never want to let her go.

Galena

Roller coaster? Check!

Trying every game with reasonable odds at the casino? Check!

Fantastic sex? *Ding! Ding! Ding!*

Now we're at a champagne bar, where you just push a button for more champagne. I take a sip of my second bubbly delight and lean sideways against Levi sitting next to me. "I'm having the best time. What a great last day of vacation."

He tips my chin up and kisses me. "You think you'll go on another looping coaster again?"

"Maybe in ten years when my nieces need their aunt to hold their hand on one."

He laughs. "You about busted my eardrum with your screaming."

"I told you that was fun screaming. Like adrenaline-pumping screams."

"You sounded terrified."

"But in a good way."

He kisses me again, and I wrap my arms around his neck, kissing him passionately. Levi is an amazing kisser.

I break the kiss, a little out of breath. "I'm thinking we should go back to our room."

He takes my hand and kisses the back of it, his eyes intent on mine. "I'm thinking you should move in with me."

I tilt my head, not quite sure I heard right. "Sorry, what?"

"I've got a house. You really want to live in a house, so why not mine?"

My brows scrunch in confusion. "I have a house."

"No, you have half a house that you share with a man you're no longer involved with."

"But I half own it. If I don't go back, he's going to think I abandoned it. A court might say he has more right to it. Therefore, I can't leave. Thank you, though." I pick up my champagne glass, ready for another long delicious drink.

"Fuck court," he snaps.

I jump and nearly spill my champagne. This whole trip Levi hasn't uttered a single harsh word. "What's wrong?"

"What's wrong is that I want to be with you, and I don't want you living with your ex."

I go for lusty distraction. "Kiss me."

"I'm being serious."

I sigh. "You can't order me out of my own house. It didn't work with Kevin, and it's not going to work with you. We've only known each other for a week."

"An intense week where we did everything together, including live together in our hotel room."

"A week. Seven days." I finish my champagne and press the button for more. "Hotel is vacation time."

"Galena."

I kiss him. "Levi."

The bartender brings by my third glass of champagne, and I beam at him. "Thank you!"

"Admit you feel something for me," Levi orders.

"I already told you I think you're wonderful and amazing." I toss back some champagne. "Stop ordering me around, please."

"It's him or me."

"That's ridiculous. I'm not even with him."

He strokes a hand up my spine, sending hot shivers through me. His hand lands on the back of my neck and squeezes. I relax even more under his touch. "I don't want to fight with you on our last day."

"Me either. I'm on my third glass of champagne, and I'd really like to enjoy this bubbly happy feeling."

He grumbles something I can't quite hear and then kisses my cheek. "Okay."

I rub his chest, enjoying the hard warmth under my hand. "Will you take me to bed? I need you again."

"Shh," he whispers in my ear.

"Sorry," I whisper back. "Will you?"

He wraps my hair around his hand and tugs. My breath stutters out. His voice rumbles near my ear. "You need me in your bed but not in your life?"

"Kiss the bride," I order.

"Galena."

I smile up at him. "Levi."

His lips hover over mine. "Do you want me in your bed but not your life?"

I don't know! I'm confused and lusty and vulnerable. Stop asking me all these difficult questions!

"I love having you in my bed," I answer honestly. "I've never experienced anything like it. Please, Levi, it's our last night of vacation."

He kisses me long and deep, and the tension between us vanishes in a rush of lust. I don't even care about the other people at the bar. Nothing matters except for the most outrageous attraction I've ever experienced in my life. It's a constant, aching pull for more. Levi awakened a raw primal need within me that I never knew existed.

He breaks the kiss and signals for the check.

I sip champagne while he pays our bill. I can't stop smiling in between sips, giddy from champagne and knowing I get to have another glorious time in bed with only the second man I've ever slept with. I'm glad Levi looks for inner beauty. Most guys can't see past my glasses. Excuse me for not wanting to deal with contacts on a daily basis.

And it's true that I'm not a fashion diva, but my clothes are clean and loose enough to be comfortable. I like to focus on my work, and constricting clothes are a distraction. My cheeks are round, very round like apples, but that's just normal for my genes. Mom has the same apple cheeks. I've been called chipmunk cheeks by some guys, which is why I never slept with them. *Their loss.*

"You see the inside of me, right, Levi? Like my mind and inner-beauty stuff."

He takes my empty glass from me and sets it on the bar. Then he cups my face in his hands. "I see all of you. A beautiful, smart, kind person."

"Aww, you too. Thank you!"

"You seem a little tipsy."

"Yup."

"Let's take a walk down the Strip before we go back to the room. I want to see it lit up at night one last time."

"Okay, but then I want to try that thing again you taught me while my mouth is nice and relaxed. I could do it better this time. Oh!"

He lifted me right off my barstool, cradled in his arms.

I pat his bicep. "You're a very strong man."

The rest is a blur as we speed through the casino, and then he sets me down, and we speed walk to our hotel. It's not far.

The moment we get back to our room, I strip him naked, push him back on the bed, and have my wicked way with him. He's a mouthful, and I try different angles until I hear him moan long and low. I knew I could be so much better at this blow job thing with practice. It's awesome to have a big strong man at my mercy.

His fingers tangle in my hair, and then he tugs, lifting me up. "You have to stop. I'm not going to last."

I huff. "But it's going great, and you know I need the practice." I go back to work, doing my best to give as much pleasure to him as he's given me. A whole new world of pleasure.

He gasps. "Galena!"

I look up at him. His expression looks nearly pained. Was I doing it wrong? I sit back on my heels. "Are you okay?"

He reaches for me. "My turn to be in control."

"But I didn't finish," I protest as he maneuvers my body into position. He turns me to lie on my stomach, facing my pillow, and then yanks my hips up.

"I want to finish inside you," he says.

I can't keep the disappointment from my voice. "How am I supposed to improve—" I gasp as he thrusts inside me.

He groans. "Brace yourself on your elbows."

As soon as I do, he thrusts hard into me and stays there while his fingers delve between my legs, stroking rapidly. My back arches, every part of me on fire. The sensations rocketing through my body put me right back on the teetering edge. *Oh my God.* I'm overwhelmed, caught underneath him. Deep pressure, fiery bursts of sensation. On and on and on. I whimper incoherently as he expertly draws me to the edge and eases me back until I'm out of my mind with need.

I push back into him, silently begging for more of his hard thrusts. I moan softly as he fills me to the hilt.

He covers me, whispering in my ear, "You're mine. I need to hear you say it."

"Levi." It's all I can manage.

His fingers are wicked, pushing me harder as he thrusts relentlessly. His voice is harsh by my ear with each thrust. "Say. You're. Mine."

I can't speak, panting as my body races to release. Fever hot, my insides coil tightly, and I tremble on the brink.

He stills, and I protest. "Please! I'm so close."

His fingers tease me, round and round, not quite touching where I need him.

"I need to hear you say it, Galena."

"I'm yours," I gasp out, and he pushes me right back to the sharp edge of release with his knowing fingers and deep thrusts.

The room goes out of focus for a moment, and then the orgasm slams into me. I shudder under him, gasping for breath as wave after wave crashes over me. He grips my hips and thrusts hard and fast, and I feel it building inside me again. Oh God.

He mutters a curse, cupping my sensitive sex as he thrusts. He lets go with a roar just as I go off, my body contracting around him. I would collapse if he weren't holding me tight. I love everything about this moment. The bone-deep satisfaction, the musky scent of sex, the sweat on our bodies.

He pulls out, and I collapse to the mattress. He collapses next to me.

Long moments later, he pulls me close. More like drags me. I'm boneless. He shifts me so I'm on my side facing him, my head resting on his chest. He's so warm I could fall asleep just like this.

He kisses my temple. "This isn't just a good time in Vegas. Not for me."

I close my eyes, nearly asleep. "Okay, love you, goodnight."

"What did you just say?"

Sleep pulls at me. Suddenly there's a bright light in my eyes. I squint against it and roll to my other side.

He props up on an elbow and leans over me. "What did you just say?"

My mind clears a bit as it hits me what I said. "I don't know. What did you hear?"

"You love me."

"It just slipped out."

He rolls me to my back. "I love you too."

"This is bad," I blurt and roll away from him. Then I casually shift closer and closer to the edge of the mattress. I shouldn't have said words I can't deliver on.

He grabs me by the hips and drags me back. What does it say about me that I'm excited? All this sex has muddled things in my mind.

I sit up in bed and face him. "I can't do this. I'm sorry."

He pushes a lock of hair behind my ear. "It's not convenient, but it's real."

"I have stuff to deal with. I'm not sure I'm ready for this. Can you give me some time?"

"No."

I'm taken aback. "Why not?"

"Because I've never felt like this before, and now that I found you, I don't want to lose you."

A shiver goes through me. Suddenly it's all too much. It was only a week ago I thought I was going to spend the rest of my life with Kevin. "This is a really intense conversation for, oh, one a.m."

"You belong with me."

"Maybe I should sleep in my own bed."

I dash out of bed before he can catch me, but then I have

to walk all the way around his bed to get to mine. I can feel his eyes on me.

He walks to the bathroom, his stride stiff.

I curl on my side in my bed, tears stinging my eyes. I didn't mean to hurt him. I'm just feeling too much too soon. I turn off the light and get under the covers. This time sleep doesn't pull at me. I keep thinking about Levi and what I should've said. And how much I wish our last night on vacation ended on a good note instead of a sour one. I toss and turn, finding it impossible to get comfortable.

And then the covers lift, and he scoots in behind me, spooning me. My entire body relaxes. In just a week, I've gotten used to sleeping in his arms. Kevin and I used to sleep at opposite ends of the bed, facing different directions. Cuddling wasn't in the mix. I need to stop comparing them. It just goes to show things happened too quickly. I should be able to think only of Levi when I'm with him. Instead Kevin haunts me.

I'm so torn. Is this an exciting new beginning with Levi, or will everything change when we get back to our lives back home? How do I know it's real? Vegas feels like a whole different world, and I'm a different person here.

Levi strokes my hair back. "I'm sorry for pushing you. I'll give you the time you need."

"Thank you," I manage over the lump in my throat. But I'm not at all sure what we had here will last in real life.

Maybe Vegas was just a fantasy world.

12

Levi

Vacation time's over, and I want to believe it's not the end, but it's not looking promising. When Galena and I parted ways at the Vegas airport, she already seemed distant. We took different flights back to New York. She's home now, and I know it's soon, but I just arrived back in town and have to see her.

I knock on the door and hear raised voices inside. Galena and her ex. His voice carries the loudest. "That's all it was! Why can't you forgive me?"

I knock harder. They're in the thick of an argument. "You're not listening!" Galena exclaims.

More yelling and accusations, mostly from him.

I pound on the door, and this time they hear me. It gets quiet, and then the door opens. Kevin, a man I only briefly saw at his wedding before he bailed, stares at me. He's a tall skinny guy with short blond hair. He's no threat to me physically; only his presence in Galena's life is a threat.

"Who are you?" he asks.

"Don't you remember me from your wedding? I'm Levi, the wedding officiant. Oh, that's right, you didn't stick around long enough to remember much."

Galena appears at the door. "Levi, now's not a good time. Kevin just got home from work."

"On a Sunday?"

"I'm close to a breakthrough in my research that could change the world," Kevin says smugly. "Why are you here?"

I look to Galena, and she shakes her head. She hasn't told him about me. He has no idea I just took *his* honeymoon in Vegas. "I wanted to make sure Galena was okay at home. Figured it could be a tense situation to share a house with someone when you're no longer together."

"We're together," he says. "Just not married."

"Kevin and I have a lot to talk about," Galena says, giving me a pointed look. "Privately."

"He left you at the altar," I say, feeling desperate.

"It was just cold feet with the magazine people," Kevin protests. "A private wedding with a national magazine there to document it. Anyone would get cold feet."

"Galena didn't," I say. "And it's not like you didn't know they'd be there."

He turns to Galena. "I'm sorry. I didn't mean to leave you alone to deal with them."

"She wasn't alone," I say. "She had me."

His head whips toward me, his eyes narrowing as he steps closer. "What do you mean she had you?"

Galena steps between us. "He gave me a ride home. Levi, you should go. I'm okay. Thanks for checking in."

Kevin puts his arm around her shoulders and guides her away from the door, kicking it shut in my face. Their voices are quiet now, and my gut tightens. So that's it? She doesn't need me anymore?

Her grandfather's words ring through my head. *She's never one to rush into anything. Sorry to say, you're a rebound to help her get over Kevin.*

I don't want to believe it. My sinking gut knows differently. It's over.

∿

Galena

This has been the week from hell. Catching up on work, missing Levi, trying to navigate around Kevin, who won't move out. I need to find a lawyer to figure out how to keep my home. It's my first one ever, and I was so proud to be able to afford it. I paid a larger percentage of the down payment. I make more money than Kevin because I work for private industry while he works for a university lab.

I was even willing to sell and divide the proceeds with him, even though I really like living here in Summerdale, but he refuses. He firmly believes that given time we'll get back together and things will go back to the way they were before —living together as a couple without being married. He's agreed to sleep in the guest room down the hall. I haven't told him about Levi. And I feel guilty even thinking about being with Levi now that we're back home because it doesn't look great that I was with someone else so soon after my relationship with Kevin.

Which is why I finally accepted Kayla's invitation to attend ladies' night at The Horseman Inn on Thursday night. She wants to help me get my mind off things and introduce me to her friends. I walk in with her, and we make our way past the front dining room and wind around to the back bar area.

"Kayla!" the women exclaim in unison.

She laughs. "Hi, ladies! Sorry I'm late."

I tense, looking at the happy group of women. This is going to be exhausting, trying to keep up with conversation with people I don't know.

"They'll love you," Kayla whispers as we walk over. "Besides, they already know about your wedding situation, so you won't need to explain."

"Great," I mutter.

"Everyone in town knows. Word spreads fast."

Kayla and I take two empty seats on the end. Two of the women are noticeably pregnant, sipping sparkling water.

Aww, there's an auburn-haired woman with a baby tucked in a sling.

I walk around to see the baby. "Hi! Who's this?"

The woman pulls the sling fabric back to reveal a content-looking child with light brown hair, sucking her thumb, and looking right at me with big brown eyes. "This is Quinn."

"Hi, Quinn!" I touch her hand, and she grips my finger. "Ooh, she's strong. How old is she?"

"Four months. I'm Sydney. I own this old place."

Kayla appears next to me. "This is my cutie niece. Sydney married my older brother, Wyatt."

I study Quinn closer. "You know what, I see the resemblance. Her eyes are the same color and shape as yours, Kayla."

"That's the Winters' genes shining through," Kayla says.

"She's got the Robinson fire," Sydney says proudly.

I play peekaboo with baby Quinn, who giggles in delight. The third time I do it, she grabs my hand and yanks it away from my face.

"She likes you," Sydney says. "Do you want to hold her?"

"I'd love to."

She slides the baby out of the sling and hands her over. I hold her upright against my chest, letting her lean on my shoulder. She's warm from the sling and her adorable yellow-striped sleeper with little smiling teddy bears. And footies! I used to love pajamas with feet when I was little. Quinn doesn't rest on my shoulder for long. She leans back to stare at me and pats my hair. The tension that's been my constant companion this week drains from me. There's nothing like holding a baby to remind you of all that's good in the world. She smells so sweet and new.

"We hate Kevin on your behalf," Sydney says.

"Agreed," Paige says. She was there as the innkeeper and wedding coordinator. She knows.

Right next to Paige is a thin blonde woman who looks as pregnant as Paige. Around six months, I think Paige mentioned.

"Did you find someone else for the magazine people to write an article about?" I ask Paige.

"We did. A recently engaged couple. They didn't have a license, so for them it was more like a dress rehearsal. They want to have a big outdoor wedding by the lake next June with the whole town invited. Between you and me, I think the groom preferred the elopement ceremony. Kind of like a his and hers version of the wedding."

"That was Skylar and Gage," Kayla informs me. "You met Skylar before when you first stopped by the inn."

My mind flashes to the man who commanded most of my attention during that first visit. I remember every delicious detail of my naked time with him. I've been running it like a dirty movie in my head every night. I wish I could stop. As if conjured from my thoughts, suddenly he's here, striding toward me. I can't tear my gaze away, my heartbeat thudding against my rib cage.

Smack!

Ow! Baby Quinn just smacked my glasses and knocked them askew.

"Quinn! No hitting," Sydney says, taking the baby from my arms. "Sorry. She's not used to glasses."

I straighten them. "No problem." My nose hurts, but that's the hazard of holding a baby. I've got a bigger hazard heading my way with a determined look.

Levi joins the group, his eyes intent on mine. The women all seem to know him, reaching out to pat his shoulder or arm as they welcome him. He spares them a quick glance and an even shorter greeting before returning his attention to me.

My throat is dry. "Hi."

"I know I have no right to make demands, but I thought we had more than just a fling."

I freeze.

The women get so quiet I can hear the bartender texting on her phone.

"Could we talk somewhere more private?" I ask.

He gestures toward the back dining room, where there's several empty tables.

"Take your pick!" Sydney says.

As we walk away, I can hear the women whispering behind us, probably speculating over me and Levi. I'm torn between throwing myself at him and running far, far away. I've never had so many conflicting emotions. Life used to be simple—predictable and easy. Until it wasn't.

I take a seat, suddenly wishing I had a drink just to occupy my hands. I cross my arms, tucking my hands tightly against me. "Levi, my life is complicated right now."

He sits in the chair adjacent to me. "So you're back with Kevin?"

"We're like roommates."

"What does that mean?"

"Separate bedrooms. Same house. We co-own it. He doesn't want to sell, and I refuse to give it up. I'm going to research lawyers this weekend."

"Move in with me."

"That's not going to happen."

"Why not?"

"First, it's way too soon to move in together. Second, that's as good as saying I give up the house. He doesn't know I was with you on what was supposed to be our honeymoon. How's that going to look to a lawyer? It'll just give Kevin more ammunition that he's the wronged party."

He clenches his jaw. "He dumped you on your wedding day. If anyone was the wronged party, it was you."

"It's about appearances."

He gives me a long searching look. Our time together in Vegas comes back to me, not just in the sexy flashes of remembrance from our time in bed. From the ease we had with each other, the laughter, the wonderful way he had with my grandparents.

"Do you remember what I told you on our last night in Vegas?" he asks.

You belong with me. The words have haunted me because I'm not ready for serious commitment.

He leans close. "I said I love you. And you said it first. That means something." He takes my hand. "Move out of the toxic situation you're in and move in with me."

"I can't."

"Then let's convince him to sell so you can both be free."

"I tried. I'll try again, okay?"

He gazes into my eyes and then gently slides my glasses off, cleaning them on his shirt. He slides them back on my face, and the world is suddenly crystal clear. "I don't mean to come on strong. I miss you."

My heart leaps in my throat. "I miss you too."

And then he kisses me, and I remember how much I love being with this man. All the tenderness, all the passion floods my senses.

Applause breaks out. I turn to find Kayla and friends clapping for us. I face front, my cheeks flaming.

He smiles. "They're happy for us. Let's go over."

He takes my hand, and it suddenly feels like we're a couple. And I know I shouldn't care about having everyone's approval of the match, but after no one was crazy about Kevin for me, it feels damn good.

Levi

Okay, I didn't get all I hoped for with our conversation, but it seems Galena is open to being with me, even though it's soon after her breakup. She's smiling as we join the women at the bar. I grew up with most of them; three of them were in my grade.

"Feel this," Jenna says, taking my hand and placing it on her pregnant belly. Jenna's a thin blonde who ironically owns the bakery in town, Summerdale Sweets. She's always been able to eat anything. Her baby belly is the only part of her that's not thin. A protruding something jabs at me. Elbow, knee?

"That's wild," I say. "How're you liking pregnancy?"

She rubs her belly, making a face at another sharp jab. "Once I got past the early stage, I liked it. They say it gets harder after this as the baby weighs down on my bladder. For now there's room for both of us."

Galena stares at the movement under Jenna's thin white shirt. "That *is* wild. I can see it moving through your shirt."

Jenna stares at her belly. "He or she gets active the moment I sit or lie down. It hasn't been easy to fall asleep."

Galena keeps staring, and Jenna grabs her hand and puts it on her belly too. Galena's jaw drops, her eyes full of wonder. This is a woman who loves babies and kids. She was holding baby Quinn close when I first got here. To think she wasn't going to have kids because Kevin didn't want them. I want to give that to her. I want to give her everything she deserves, but she's not entirely mine. I hate that she still lives with him. How easy would it be to fall into old patterns? Two years is a long time to be with someone.

"My baby moves too," Paige announces. "But don't even think about touching my belly."

"She's sensitive," Kayla says.

Not how Paige strikes me, but her sister Kayla would know.

"We're both due in September," Jenna says. "It's so nice to have someone to go through this with at the same time. Our kids can play together, grow up together."

"Quinn will be playdate leader," Sydney chimes in.

Audrey stares at the bar. Jenna, Sydney, and Audrey have been tight since elementary school. It's impossible not to notice she's left out.

I shift over to Audrey at the far end of the bar, bringing Galena with me. "Hey, Audrey. This is Galena Torres. She recently moved to town. Galena, Audrey Fox, our town librarian and local author."

"Nice to meet you," Galena says. "What have you written?"

Audrey shakes her head. "Not an author yet."

"She's writing, though," I say. "It's a multigenerational saga about a soldier with PTSD and her family's history in the military."

"Wow, that must've taken a lot of research," Galena says.

Drew Robinson rises from the corner table he usually takes by the bar and joins us. He's the oldest in the Robinson family, owner of a karate dojo in town, and a former Army ranger. A man of few words with a manner that can best be described as stealth assassin. "I helped her with that. I read a lot of military histories and biographies."

Audrey rolls her eyes. "Yes, he likes to remind me of that, even though I know how to research as a librarian." They've had this conversation before at some of our Winterfest meetings. There's a weird dynamic between them. Growing up, Audrey worshipped him—even I heard about it. She wrote him daily emails when he was on overseas missions. Now she's a bit edgy with him, and somehow that's made him more interested in conversation.

Now that I think about it, they were discussing her book back in January, which she'd already been working on for some time. It's June now.

"Are you close to finishing your book?" I ask Audrey.

"I finished it," she says quietly.

"You should send it to publishers," Drew says. "Get it out there."

She gives him a skeptical look. "It's not ready. I haven't even let anyone read it."

"I'll read it," he says.

"Go for it," Jenna calls over. "It's not like he hasn't read plenty of your words before."

Only a lifelong friend would dare throw that out there. Jenna's reminding her of all the emails Audrey wrote Drew. This was way back in middle school. Drew's five years older than us.

"Careful, Jenna," Audrey says, baring her teeth in a scary smile. "I'm a yellow belt now."

Jenna puts her hands on her pregnant belly protectively. "You wouldn't karate chop a pregnant woman, would you?"

"I'll wait until you have the baby, and then when you least expect it—payback." Audrey sounds serious.

Jenna's eyes widen. "Sorry, I was just kidding. Someone should read your work, Aud. Otherwise, why did you spend more than a year writing it? This is your baby."

Audrey mumbles, "Yeah."

Galena catches my eye. Yeah, I noticed that too. Audrey's the only one of the three friends missing out on the baby experience.

Drew stares at Audrey. "It would be an honor to read your book."

Audrey meets his eyes briefly and then stares at the bar. "It's not ready."

He leans on the bar, dipping his head to meet her eyes. "When it's ready. Next month, okay?"

Audrey shakes her head.

He taps the bar. "I'm not letting this go."

She gives him a wry look. "At least you're talking to me again. And actually looking me in the eye. Got over your shock?"

I actually know what she's talking about. Three weeks ago, we were all at Skylar and Gage's engagement party, and General Joan was calling for Audrey. She and Drew stepped out of the kitchen together. Audrey's face was pink, and Drew looked shocked. I've never seen the man look like that before.

Drew clears his throat and pulls at the collar of his T-shirt. "I'm trying to help you get your book out in the world."

Audrey turns to Galena. "So tell me, how did you and Levi become a thing?"

The women chime in with a chorus of questions about me and Galena. Drew slips away, moving back to his corner table, where he likes to watch the Yankees on the TV above the bar. He probably wants the company of the bar while still having space to himself at that table. Or maybe he's on the lookout for Audrey. She works within walking distance and often stops by.

"We're not a thing," Galena says emphatically.

"We're definitely a thing," I say. "I went to Vegas with her last week."

"Ooh!" the women say in near unison.

Galena's fingers flutter in the air. "It was already arranged and paid for. My grandparents live in Las Vegas."

"Tell them how I pretended to be your husband for the wedding party your grandparents threw for us at their house."

"No!" Kayla exclaims. "Galena, how could you not tell me this? I had lunch with you twice this week. No wonder you don't want to leave your desk. You've got all this fantastic drama going on in your life! Levi's awesome. I couldn't be happier for you two."

"Thank you, Kayla," I say.

"It's complicated," Galena says weakly.

"We all hate your ex, and we love Levi," Sydney says. "I'm with Kayla. Go for it."

"Yeah," the women chime in.

"Peer pressure," I whisper to Galena. "Remember when everyone said 'kiss the bride,' and all the pressure made us give in to the inevitable? Remember how good it feels between us?"

She flushes and turns to the bartender. "Can I get a drink?"

"It's Thursday Night Wine Club," Sydney says. "Get her a glass of that awesome chardonnay."

"It's supposed to be Thursday Night Book Club," Audrey says to Galena. "But they never read the book. Would you like to join me at book club at the library next Tuesday? We could use some younger people there."

"I'm not sure I'll have time to read that fast," Galena says.

"Next one, then. Let me know your number so I can text you about it."

Galena shares her number, smiling shyly. "I've been hoping to meet more people in town. Where I used to live, I didn't know anyone. It was an apartment, and I was hardly ever home anyway with work and spending time with my nieces."

"Welcome to Summerdale," Audrey says. "No escape."

Galena laughs and presses against my side. This is a very good sign.

13

———

Galena

This is a very bad sign. Levi wants to pick up where we left off in Vegas, and it feels like too much too fast. Vegas was vacation. This is real life. He leaves the bar with me, his hand on the small of my back in a heated imprint I well remember.

"I'll walk you home," he says.

"Not necessary." My house is only a block away, and I feel like I could use the time to clear my head before dealing with Kevin at home. I've never had to manage two demanding men at the same time. I don't know which is more difficult to deal with—the one who wants my heart back or the one who stole it.

He smiles. "I know it's not necessary. I want to."

I stop near the one streetlight in the parking lot and look up at him. "It's not a good idea."

"Why? Because of Kevin?"

"Yes."

"So you still haven't told him about us?"

I cross my arms. "Not yet."

"Then let's go tell him now. Together."

"I need more time to convince him to sell our house. He's not going to leave, and it's the only way I can recoup my investment and ever be able to afford another house."

"I hate to break it to you, but what happened back there —" he gestures toward The Horseman Inn behind us "— means the news is out. Those ladies will spread the word faster than you can say Las Vegas. They've probably already texted their husbands about us, and any other friends who couldn't make it tonight. This is small town life. Word travels fast, especially juicy news about their mayor. I haven't had one scandal my entire career. Me going on your honeymoon with you is irresistible catnip to them."

"You're comparing women to cats?"

"I'm just saying the word is out, so you'd better tell Kevin."

"He barely speaks to anyone in town except when he picks up takeout. I'm sure he won't find out."

"But what if he sees us together?"

I hesitate. Part of me wants to be with him, but the wiser part of me is screaming caution. My heart's on the line, and I don't know if it can handle any more damage. That's what all this comes down to. It's not just the mess with Kevin and the house. I'm still recovering from heartbreak. How can I risk opening my heart again? Levi's not playing around here. He wants more from me.

Levi tips my chin up. "Galena?"

I back away. "I need more time. It's complicated, and I have a lot to figure out."

"What do you need to figure out?"

I hold up a palm. "I'm going now. Bye."

"I can help you with the house problem with your ex," he says. "I'm constantly solving problems for people in town."

I hurry away, trying to outrun my own desire to let him do that for me. I need to stand on my own two feet. "Bye!"

The next day after work I come home to an empty house and let out a breath of relief. Talking to Kevin about our relationship is exhausting. He wants to constantly rehash it. As far as

I'm concerned, there's nothing more to talk about. Last night when I got home, he'd prepared a PowerPoint presentation on the pros and cons of us getting back together. The pros won of course, according to him. And trying to forge an equitable arrangement for our house is like talking to a stone wall.

It's Friday night, and that means I can relax. My new take on life is to leave room for downtime. I don't always want to be about work like I used to be. Like Kevin still is. Anyway, it's a long holiday weekend for the Fourth of July, and Kayla invited me to go to the town fair with her tomorrow. There's a parade, tag sale, and games for the kids. I invited my sister and nieces to join us. I'd really like to feel like Summerdale's home for me the way it is for Kayla. She moved here from New Jersey after getting dumped on her wedding day too.

Kayla and I are like twins leading parallel lives. Both dumped on our wedding day, both the youngest in our family, both biostatisticians. Guess that would explain why she couldn't stop hugging me on my ruined wedding day. I nearly forgot about her similar experience in my time of distress. Now Kayla has a doting, gorgeous husband, and I have…a mess.

I putter around the kitchen, not up to cooking but hungry. I pull out crackers, peanut butter, and jelly. Dinner of champions. It's comfort food. As I'm eating them, I think about what I'll do next. Maybe I'll make popcorn and watch a movie.

The doorbell rings, followed by a high-pitched howl. Now who would stop by with their dog? Kayla's dog, Tank, rarely makes a noise above a snuffle. Nerves race through me because part of me knows. It must be him.

I go to the door, peek through the peephole, and open it. Butterflies dance in my stomach the moment our eyes meet. This only happens with Levi.

He smiles at me, his dog, Baxter, lunging to sniff my fingers. "Down, boy," Levi orders, pulling him back.

I laugh a little, glad for the distraction. "My hands probably smell like peanut butter. I just had peanut butter and jelly on crackers for dinner." I smooth my hair back self-consciously and then worry I got peanut butter in my hair. I glance down at my old souvenir T-shirt from a theme park and black sweatpants. Not exactly dressed to impress.

I meet his warm brown eyes and feel myself melting. "I wasn't expecting company."

"I'm not company. Next time call me before you resort to peanut butter and jelly for dinner. I'm sure I can do better. I make a mean fettuccini alfredo."

"Impressive. I make a mean omelet. So, uh, what're you doing here?"

"Taking Baxter for his walk. Want to join us? We're going around the lake."

"Uh, sure. Let me just get my sneakers."

"Can we come in?"

I back up and gesture for them to come in. "Just be a minute."

"Kevin home?" he asks as I'm on my way to the stairs.

"No, he's still at work," I say and dash upstairs. I grab my socks and sneakers, and then I rethink my outfit. Do I really want to walk around the lake with the mayor of Summerdale in sweatpants? We're sure to run into people he knows, and he'll introduce me. I change into fitted black shorts and then go to the bathroom mirror to brush my hair. I had taken it out of its bun after work, and it's sort of rumpled.

I look closer in the mirror at something red on the side of my mouth. *Great.* There's a spot of jelly. Would he have mentioned it? Would he have brushed it away with his finger, or licked it away? Heat rushes through me as memories of Levi flood my mind.

I give myself a hard look in the mirror. *Be sensible. Vegas was an outlier from normal life that can't be repeated until you're sure your heart is healed and Kevin is completely out of the picture.*

Why couldn't I have met Levi under different circumstances a year from now? Even six months would've been better. Timing matters.

He *was* there for me when I needed someone. I just never thought I'd get so tangled up with him so fast. Vegas accelerated everything between us. What was I thinking with that spontaneous invite? Welp, the genie's out of the bottle. But what do I wish?

I add some cherry red lip gloss just to look presentable to my neighbors. I'm *not* trying to impress Levi. Okay, socks and shoes. I place a hand over my chest. *Why is my heart racing?*

I put on my socks with shaking hands. Adrenaline. That's all. The stakes are high, and I'm pulling a balancing act here between heart and mind. Not to mention my traitorous body.

I lace up my sneakers and hurry downstairs. "Hi."

"Hi, beautiful."

My face flushes. "Stop. I'm not." I cross to Levi, my eyes on Baxter. "Who's a good beagle?"

"Who says you're not?" Levi asks softly.

I look up at him. He searches my expression before tucking a lock of hair behind my ear, his fingers grazing my cheek, bringing warmth and another rush of memories. Levi can be tender in a way I've never experienced before and, at the same time, demanding in a way that makes me weak with pleasure.

I back up a step. "I don't think you look too closely at me. You didn't even notice I had jelly on my face earlier."

He steps into my personal space, pinches my chin, and kisses me. Just a peck but I instantly want more. "I thought you were saving that bit for later."

I smooth my hair behind my ears, suddenly awkward. "Right."

"I was just happy to see you and didn't make a close examination. Honestly, I think you'd look beautiful wearing a sack."

Now I know he's just being nice. "Okay, I'll remember to look for a sack next time I go shopping." I open the door and step out, locking it behind us.

We head down the porch steps and to the front walk.

"Did you tell Kevin about Vegas?" he asks the moment we reach the street.

I sigh. "It's only been a day since you asked me to do that

and no. I haven't seen him. Last night he got home after I went to bed, and I left this morning while he was in the shower. He's not home from work yet and will probably work late again. He's all about work."

"All work and no play makes a dull boy."

"That used to be me, but I've got a new take on life. I'm trying to leave more room for fun."

"Then that means you have room for me." Baxter bumps my hand with his muzzle as if to remind me he wants in on the fun too. "And Baxter," he says with a laugh.

I laugh too, keeping the focus on his playful beagle. "I washed my hands, but they must still smell like peanut butter to him."

"How was your week? Getting back into the swing of things?"

I'm so relieved that he's not pressing me about Kevin, or what Levi and I are to each other after Vegas that I spill everything about work. How there's a new treatment for Alzheimer's that we're excited about, and the data looks very promising.

We reach the lake, and I stop mid-conversation to take in the breathtaking beauty of the rippling water surrounded by tall trees in their full greenery. A few rowboats and sailboats are out on the lake, little kids splashing close to shore. Someone's throwing a Frisbee to their black lab, who's diving into the water after it. The air here smells so fresh and clean. I half want to run into the water and splash around for the sheer joy of it. How crazy is that?

"Hi, guys!" Kayla calls, pulling a red wagon behind her. She's with her husband, Adam.

I smile. "Hi! Hey, Adam." Her husband is a tall lean guy with dark brown hair and a scruffy jaw. He always looks serious except when he looks at Kayla. Then he looks enthralled.

"Hey," Adam says. "How's it going?"

When we reach them, I get a closer look at the wagon, where Tank, an English bulldog, sits under a shade with a fan blowing on him. Kayla talks about Tank all the time like he's her baby. She refers to her cat Simba as his little sister.

"Things are going well," Levi says. "Getting ready for the Fourth of July events. Will you be there?"

"Absolutely," Kayla says. "Galena's meeting us at the fair tomorrow with her sister and nieces."

"Is that so?" Levi nudges my arm. "I'm looking forward to meeting them."

"Her nieces are so cute!" Kayla gushes. "Galena's like a second mom to them."

"Just an aunt," I say.

"And godmother," Kayla says. "You're so good with them." She beams. "Adam and I are trying."

Adam coughs, a faint pink on his neck. "Kayla, that's private."

I stifle a laugh and exchange an amused look with Levi. Kayla is a major oversharer, and her husband is just the opposite, extremely reserved and private.

Kayla grabs his hand and squeezes it. "Sorry, I'm just so excited. We don't officially start until tonight. I realized this was the night when I got home, but then we had to take Tank on his walk first."

Levi looks over at Tank lounging in his red wagon. "Yes, it looks like his legs are getting quite a workout."

She laughs. "We have a deal. He walks on the way to the lake, and then he can ride in the wagon on the way back."

"She spoils him," Adam says.

She shoots him a look. "Adam used to carry him home. Talk about spoiling. Tank is much too heavy for that."

Adam flexes his bicep. Kayla pats his bicep and returns back to her oversharing topic. "I read up on the proper timing for conception—"

"More than they need to know, sweetheart," Adam says.

Kayla's eyes meet mine with her excited *I have so much to share* look. I'm sure she'll tell me all the research she's done into the best way to conceive when I see her at work on Monday. I've heard way more than I ever needed to know from her about many intimate subjects. That's Kayla for you.

I give her a slight nod, indicating we'll talk later about the details. "I'm looking forward to my first town fair." I turn to Levi. "Kayla told me about all the different fairs, festivals, and celebrations in town."

"Oh, yeah, seems like they're multiplying," Levi says with a sigh. "I'm always at one meeting or another, coordinating the effort. It's good for the community, but it's a ton of work. We depend entirely on volunteers. Maybe you'd like to join a committee."

"I avoid committees and meetings at all costs," I say, repressing a shudder.

"It'll be fun," Kayla says. "I always do the pancake breakfast with Santa. You should do it with us this year, Galena. We help with the kids and dance together."

"Dressed like an elf," Adam puts in helpfully.

I cringe.

"In a cute way," Kayla assures me. "The kids love it."

"Maybe I'll bring my nieces to it."

"We'll talk about it more when it gets closer." Kayla gestures to me and Levi. "So great to see you two."

I worry my lower lip. The ladies' night group believes we're a couple, and now we're out on a walk together with oversharing Kayla as a witness for our second time together in two days. Word's going to spread like wildfire. I have to sit down with Kevin and tell him what's up. I'm not even sure about a future with Levi, but there's no denying we had something in Vegas.

Tank lets out his quiet *oof* bark, his eyes bulging wide, as Baxter scrambles into the wagon with him. I crack up. Baxter looks so pleased with himself. He's hogging the fan, panting into it, his big floppy ears fluttering back.

"Oh no," Kayla says. "Tank doesn't like to share his wagon. He growls when I put a teddy bear in it."

Levi scoops up Baxter, who scrambles to get out of his

arms and back in the wagon. Levi wins the struggle and sets him down a distance away.

Kayla wiggles her fingers at us. "We'd better go. I'll see you both at the fair. Galena, let's meet by Summerdale Sweets at eleven for a primo spot for the parade. We can get ice-cream sandwiches. Jenna makes them with cake layers, and they're so good! I'm sure your nieces will love them too."

"I'll be there."

We say our goodbyes and continue on. I hear Kayla exclaim to Adam as they walk away, "Aren't they a cute couple?"

I risk a sideways look at Levi.

He's smiling. "Adam calls her a force of nature."

"Lots of energy, that's for sure." Part of me wants to address the couple thing, and part of me likes having the approval. No one approved of me and Kevin, and I know that was mostly because we were living together before marriage, and they didn't want to know him, but my sister met him and didn't like him. I always felt she didn't understand Kevin. He's a genius, and his research will probably be incredibly important to the entire world. At least that's what I always reminded myself when I wanted more from him than he could give.

Damn, I was the woman behind the man. I don't like that at all. And to think I almost spent my entire life like that.

"What're you thinking about?" Levi asks.

"My ex," I admit. "I just realized I gave him absolute support because I believed he was a genius who'd do great things, yet I never thought about myself. Maybe I need support too. Not absolute support, just—"

"Being more like a team."

"Yes. Like we're on the same team."

"I have an idea for getting your ex on board with selling the house. I need to get a few things in place first and get back to you. How's that sound to you?"

"Seems like the only equitable out is for us to sell. I'll miss Summerdale, though."

He winks. "I'm sure we can find you a place to stay."

"Levi, it's way too soon to even consider that."

"I get it. I can keep an eye out for houses that go up for sale. This is a good time of year to sell. A lot of families move here for our school district, and they like to move in the summer before school starts."

"If you can make it work, I'm open to selling."

"Excellent."

We continue our walk around the lake, talking like old friends. Levi's so easy to talk to. I guess it goes back to his awesome people skills. We're stopped several times by people who want a word with him about a variety of town issues, from tree branches near electrical wires to lawn-mowing times on the weekend to enforcing the leash law. I did notice there's a lot of dog owners here. Except for the lab running into the lake, I've only ever seen them on a leash.

We finish our walk and head back toward my street.

Levi gives me a sheepish grin. "My work follows me."

"That's okay. It was interesting. You have to be diplomatic to be fair to everyone, even when you have to say no."

"It's a balancing act."

"I admire what you do. You're like the beating heart of the community just walking around."

He laughs. "That's one way to put it."

Baxter lunges ahead after a deer tiptoeing through a side yard. Levi holds him back. "Leave it." He struggles with the leash, as Baxter's determined to get to the deer, who's frozen in place.

"This is why I switched to a harness," Levi tells me. "So pulling on the leash won't choke him." He gives a tug and rushes past the yard with Baxter dragging behind him.

I keep up with them, walking quickly.

Levi whistles a jaunty tune to distract Baxter, who keeps looking back over his shoulder.

He's good with his dog. He's good with everyone. Why am I holding back with him?

I look up as a familiar black Mazda zips past me and pulls

into the driveway of my house. "I should go. Have a good night."

"Is that Kevin?" Levi asks.

Kevin gets out of the car and looks down the street at us. "What's up?"

Guess there's no getting around this awkward moment. Kevin spotted us, and Levi's striding forward with Baxter.

"How ya doing, neighbor," Levi says. "I live a block over."

Kevin looks at me and then back to Levi. "This is the second time I've seen you at my house. Are you two together?"

"It's complicated," I blurt.

"Yes," Levi says.

Kevin puts his hands on his slim hips. "What's going on?"

"Kevin, we should talk inside," I say.

"Just tell me now," he says. "Seems like less than two weeks since our wedding, and you're already with another guy."

"It's not like that," I say. "We're friends."

"Seriously?" Levi says.

Baxter sniffs Kevin's pant leg and tries to climb his leg. Kevin shakes him off. "Keep your dog off me."

Levi gives Baxter a tug back and orders him to sit. Baxter sits for a moment and then goes to me for attention. I give him a scratch behind the ear. "See you later," I tell Baxter and then look up at Levi, including him in the goodbye. *Uh-oh.* Levi and Kevin are having a staredown. I don't think Kevin would ever get into a physical altercation, but he looks really angry.

"Why does *our* wedding officiant keep showing up at *our* house?" Kevin asks me, never taking his eyes off Levi.

"You broke up with her," Levi snaps. "On her wedding day. I went to Vegas with her."

Kevin recoils like he's been slapped. "What! No, that doesn't sound right. Galena would never go away with a stranger."

"It's true, Kevin. I was going to tell you. Can we talk inside? I'll explain everything."

Kevin stares at me for a long moment. His lip curls. "Everything is crystal clear. You'd never go off with a stranger. You must've been together before that." He shakes his head. "I never would've pegged you as a cheater."

"I'm not, I swear. This was all spontaneous in the aftermath of our breakup."

Kevin crosses his arms. "Levi, you're not welcome in our house. Stay away." He walks inside.

I glance at Levi. His jaw is clenched. Baxter whines at his side.

"Bye," I whisper before heading inside. There's nothing more to say. Now everyone knows everything, and my life is still complicated as hell with two angry men on my hands, and I can't please either of them.

I need time to recover, time to think about what I really need to move forward with my life. I just hope I don't lose what could potentially be a great relationship in the meantime.

Kevin nearly runs into me on his way out. "I'm going to pick up dinner and head back to the lab."

"Okay."

The door slams shut behind him. I stand there for a moment, my mind a whirl of conflicting emotions. Maybe I should stop by Levi's house just to be sure he's okay.

14

The next day as I walk down the street toward the fair-grounds with my sister and nieces, I keep running into people I've met through Levi or from ladies' night at The Horseman Inn. It's awesome, and I'm flying high feeling like I'm part of the Summerdale community. Okay, full confession, I'm in a good mood because Levi and I hooked up last night. I know, I know, things are complicated, and I'm still an emotional mess, but—

It. Was. Amazing.

Out-of-control, urgent intensity. Like all that sexual tension from not hooking up since Vegas exploded. I flush hot in memory.

My sister elbows me. "Looks like you landed in a good place. You already know a bunch of people." Izzy's four years older and beautiful—glossy brown hair with no frizz whatsoever, perfect skin, and somehow she got a rare tall gene in our family that makes her look like a model. She never even needed glasses. Not that I'm jealous. Growing up, maybe a little. I always consoled myself that I was better at school. Now that stuff doesn't matter so much.

"It's starting to feel like home," I say.

"Except for the ex fouling up your space."

"What's ex?" my six-year-old niece Grace asks.

Izzy and I burst out laughing. With Grace's missing front teeth, it sounds like, "What's sex?" (with an adorable lisp).

Grace purses her lips. "What's so funny?"

"Nothing, sweetie," I say. "Your mom was talking about my old boyfriend. He's called my ex-boyfriend now because he's not my boyfriend anymore. Ex for short."

"Kevin," Grace says. "He's the ex fouling up your space." My nieces met him briefly, and Kevin spoke to them like adults, saying, "It's nice to meet you." He didn't attempt to interact with them any further and was stiff the entire visit. Later, he told me he wasn't comfortable around kids because they're noisy and have no reasoning skills. At the time I thought it made sense that he didn't want kids since he clearly didn't enjoy being around them, but now it seems like a red flag. He knew how much my nieces meant to me. He could've at least tried to be friendlier.

"Where's the ice cream?" four-year-old Amelia asks, rushing ahead toward the fairgrounds, where there's tents set up for barbecue from The Horseman Inn, as well as a baked goods stand from Summerdale Sweets.

"Let's go to the bouncy house!" Grace says, jumping up and down.

I point across the street. "Over there is where they keep all the ice cream. Summerdale Sweets. After we meet my friend Kayla there, we can do the bouncy house and games."

"Yay!" the girls chorus in unison.

"If that's okay with your mom," I add. Izzy says when I'm around the girls, they defer to me like I'm the mom, and she might as well take a vacation. She never sounds too torn up about it.

"What she said," Izzy replies drily.

Summerdale's "downtown" is super cute with Summerdale Sweets in a central location on a long winding road called Peaceable Lane. There's also a library, a post office, a small grocery store, The Horseman Inn, and two churches at opposite ends of the street. Kayla told me I'd have to cross the state line into nearby Clover Park, Connecticut, for the Catholic church. These two churches are Episcopalian and Presbyterian. Kayla shops in Clover Park frequently, and she's still friendly with her wedding planner who lives there, even though Kayla's wedding was more than a year ago. She's really good about keeping in touch with people. I'll probably have to check out Clover Park with her, especially the bookstore she raves about.

"This place is darling!" Izzy exclaims as we reach Summerdale Sweets. "I love the sign and the awnings."

A painted red wooden sign over the door reads Summerdale Sweets in white letters. I haven't seen this place up close before. There's dark green awnings over large picture windows and two park benches out front. The shop is on the street level of a white square building.

I approach the front door when it opens suddenly with a cheerful jingle. Levi steps out. My heart beats double time. I haven't told Izzy about Levi. I feel guilty for being with him so soon after my breakup and loving it. At least the easy naked part.

"Hey, you," he says warmly to me. "Kayla said she's running a little late. Tank had some stomach upset, and she took him to the vet. She'll text you when she gets to the fair."

"Okay, thanks. Good to see you." My entire body flushes hot despite my casual words.

His dark eyes heat like he's also remembering every single glorious moment. I can't seem to look away, hot flashes of memory setting every nerve ending on edge. I want more.

I can feel Izzy staring, and I glance at her. Izzy's staring directly at Levi, mouth agape. I probably should've mentioned him. We didn't say we'd meet up today, but he is the mayor. Town events are kind of his thing.

Izzy speaks out of the side of her mouth. "Uh, Galena, who is this man looking at you like you're the next Miss America?"

"I could be Miss America!" Grace says, tossing her hair over her shoulder.

Amelia joins in, mimicking her sister. She's in pigtails, so her hair doesn't have quite the same effect when she tosses it over her shoulder.

Levi offers Izzy his hand. "I'm Levi Appleton. And you must be Galena's sister, Izzy. I see the family resemblance."

"I am," she says, shaking his hand. She looks delighted with him. Maybe because he's not Kevin? Or it could be his awesome people skills.

"These are my nieces, Amelia and Grace," I say, drawing the girls close, one under each arm.

"Let me guess, Amelia," he says, pointing at the right girl. "And you must be Grace."

"Yes!" the girls exclaim, delighted he picked them out correctly. I may talk about them excessively. I'm just so proud of them. Amelia's already reading at four years old, and she's so kind, always sharing treats and toys with her sister, whether or not Grace wants half a cookie that's been bitten into. Ha! And Grace is also so caring and reading at a third-grade level. Not bad for a soon-to-be first grader. I do spend a lot of time reading with the girls. Oh, and their mom probably helps too.

Levi smiles at the girls. "Who wants ice-cream sand-wiches? My treat."

"I do!" Grace shouts.

Amelia jumps up and down. "Me too!"

"Then what are we waiting for? Let's go!" He holds the door open for them, and they dash inside. He continues holding the door for me and my sister. The girls rush to the glass case with the ice cream, checking out all the flavors. Levi joins them, asking what flavors they like. He's clearly comfortable with kids. Why am I not surprised? He's good with all ages.

Izzy pulls me back by the arm. "Okay, who is that guy?"

I glance at Levi, uncomfortable revealing too much when he's nearby. "The mayor."

"And?"

"He was the officiant for my wedding that didn't happen."

"Okay, I'm sensing there's a story here."

A crazy story about how I invited the man to go on my honeymoon with me, celebrated a fake wedding reception at our grandparents' house, had wild sex, and then returned home a hot mess? That kind of story?

"We should talk later," I say.

But Izzy isn't done. "He's way into you, and vice versa. I can't believe you didn't tell me about him."

"It's only been a week."

She gives me a look that says *spill everything, girl!*

"Okay, two weeks. He went with me to Vegas."

"What!"

Levi turns back toward us. "You ladies want ice-cream sandwiches too?"

"Yes," I say, joining them.

Izzy follows me, whispering, "I want details!"

"Later," I whisper back.

She smiles sweetly at Levi and then orders for the girls. Levi gestures to the cashier. "We're all together. I've got it."

A few minutes later, we're sitting at two round tables in the shop. Levi pulled a table close so it's like one big table.

The girls are quiet, absorbed in licking the ice cream around the edges of their ice-cream cake sandwiches. They both got chocolate cake. Amelia got chocolate ice cream, and Grace got peanut butter, and they keep licking each other's to determine which one is the superior flavor. So cute. I let them try my mint ice cream chocolate sandwich too.

A brunette woman in her forties walks into the shop and heads straight for us. She's in a light yellow blouse and blue skirt with sandals, but she has the air of a woman wearing a power suit.

Levi gestures for her to join us and pulls a chair over from another table. "Carla, thanks for meeting us on your day off. This is Galena, the one I told you about. Galena, this is Carla Smith. She's a real estate lawyer. I thought she could help you out with your house problem. She's local, even though she works in the city." New York City being the only city people refer to around here.

My jaw drops. Levi could've mentioned he set up this meeting. I'd been researching lawyers, but then I decided to first try to convince Kevin the value in selling by showing how the property has already appreciated, according to my online research. He would be more swayed by numbers than lawyer threats. I've got the numbers. I just needed a good time to sit down with him.

Carla, a brunette with a short bob of hair, flashes a smile. "Hi, nice to meet you, Galena. I can see you're busy with family. Here's my card. When you get a moment, email me with more of the details for your case, and we can go from there."

Izzy chimes in, "Her ex forfeited all rights to that house when he decided not to marry her on their wedding day."

"I'm going to get married on the beach!" Grace says.

"Grace hogs the veil," Amelia says, scowling at her big sister. The girls like to play wedding with their mom's old veil and a white nightgown.

I appreciate the girls' banter at the moment because being a jilted bride caught in a war over a house that's at least half mine, if not more, is a touchy subject. I did put down sixty percent of the down payment. Levi puts a reassuring hand on my back in a show of support.

The bell jingles over the front door as someone enters the shop. It's been pretty quiet in here since most people are at the fair. I look up, and my heart jumps to my throat. Kevin's here. He actually took the day off. He's in an old T-shirt and jeans that sag on his thin frame, his blond hair is a little askew, and he's sporting his day-off scruff on his jaw. I used to find that scruff appealing. Now I look into his cool blue eyes and see only the man who won't get out of my life.

"Speak of the devil," Izzy says.

Kevin walks over to me, ignoring everyone else. "I saw you through the window. I took today off."

No kidding. Can you leave now? I really don't want a scene.

Izzy doesn't like Kevin, he doesn't like Levi, and the last thing I want is for Kevin to know I'm talking to a lawyer. That's how things escalate beyond reason. I'm starting to see the unreasonable side of Kevin, and it's impossible to deal with.

Izzy jerks a thumb at Kevin, saying to Carla, "This is the guy who won't vacate the premises even though he's been asked politely many times."

Carla nods. "Unmarried couples jointly owning property is complicated, legally speaking."

Izzy throws a hand up. "Another point for selling."

"Wait, you hired a lawyer?" Kevin asks me.

"We're just talking about the situation," I say.

Kevin's face flushes red. "You went behind my back to sic a lawyer on me?"

I try to speak calmly even though my heart's pounding. "No, it's not like that. We just met, and I was still—"

He cuts me off. "I won't be forced out of our home." He storms out.

I'm frozen in place. It's the worst-case scenario played out in front of my eyes. If Levi hadn't sprung this lawyer thing on me in a public place, none of this would've happened. Now Kevin and I will be at war. He'll probably get a lawyer too. And here I thought today would be a fun drama-free day.

Carla stands. "Get in touch when you're ready. I understand it's a difficult situation."

I nod woodenly.

Levi leans close to me. "You need a lawyer. It's the only way to get rid of him."

"He's right," Izzy says.

I frown. "In the meantime, we're both paying lawyer bills. By the time it's settled, I won't have any money left to buy a new house."

"You'll get something out of it," Izzy says.

Levi's phone dings, and he checks it. "I have to go launch the parade. I'll catch up with you later. Nice meeting you all. Enjoy your ice cream, girls." He hands Amelia a napkin, who quickly wipes her mouth and goes right back to eating the last bit of ice-cream sandwich.

"Nice meeting you too," Izzy says with a smile.

I can't bring myself to smile. "Bye."

He gives me a quizzical look before turning and walking out the door.

"I like him," Izzy says as she wipes ice-cream drippings from the table with several napkins. The girls just finished with their ice cream and are back at the ice-cream case in deep discussion over what flavors they want next time.

"Why, just because he bought us ice cream?"

"*No-o-o*. He seems like a good guy, he gives back to the community and, Galena, the way he looks at you. Like you're the best thing since sliced bread."

I roll my eyes.

"And you look at him that way too. You never looked at Kevin like that."

I sigh. "He's a good guy, though I'm not happy he sprang a lawyer on me today. He could've mentioned it. I was with him last night."

"*Ooh*, tell all."

I flush and bluster on with the important part where Levi's concerned. "I'm just not sure I'm ready to jump into a relationship. I'm still trying to get untangled from the last one. It was only two weeks ago I was about to get married."

"Major baggage, and that baggage is currently living with you. That would put a damper on anyone's love life. Though you did have Vegas…" She trails off, waiting for me to fill in the blank.

I lean close to whisper, "It was amazing! After Kevin dumped me at the wedding, I realized all my careful calculations and planning had done zilch for me. I wanted to be Galena 2.0. You know, impulsive, adventurous—"

"Fun! Good for you."

"So I impulsively invited Levi to join me in Vegas, and he did! Grandmom and Grandpop had a surprise wedding reception set up for me at their house with their friends, and things just snowballed from there. They love him."

"And you shared the honeymoon suite."

"With two beds."

"Uh-huh. I'm sure that was a big deterrent."

"He told me he loved me. After a week!"

She piles all the dirty napkins inside a clean one and balls it up. "I think when you get to a certain age and you've dated enough people, you just know when it's right. Do you love him too?"

I squirm in my seat, a bubble of excitement rising within me. "I think so, but how can I be sure—"

"No buts. That's all you need to know."

She throws out the napkins and returns to the table, putting her purse over her shoulder. The girls are still excitedly picking out ice-cream flavors for next time.

I stand and cross to her. "I'm scared about diving into the deep end again."

She hugs me. "Oh, honey. Of course you are. I'd be worried about you if you weren't. Everyone's scared in the beginning, unsure if they can trust someone with their heart, but it's exciting too, right?"

"More like terrifying."

After taking my nieces to play games for a while, we finally let them loose on the bounce house. Never let a kid bounce after eating. Parenting 101 right there. Kayla joined us for a bit, but she was worried about Tank and rushed home to check on him. When the girls' time's up in the bounce house, Grace climbs out first and helps her sister safely to the ground.

"Did you see how high I jumped?" Amelia asks us. "My pigtails jumped too!"

I laugh. "So high!"

"C'mere, let me fix your pigtail," Izzy says. She

straightens the hair band while Amelia nearly vibrates with excitement.

"I did a flip!" Grace says.

"Me too!" Amelia says, copying her big sister.

"Did not!" Grace returns, and they take off running.

"Walk!" Izzy commands.

The girls slow to a skip and make a sharp right turn around the Presbyterian church annex. We hurry to catch up with them.

"Oh no," Izzy says under her breath.

We join the girls at a white tent shading animal crates holding cats and dogs. A handsome guy, probably early thirties, in blue scrubs with short dark hair and a scruffy jaw, holds a white and black Boston terrier against his chest. The dog has an interesting face—black except for a white streak from the middle of his forehead to his nose and muzzle. His eyes are big, his nose and upper jaw short. A little like Tank's pushed-in bulldog face.

When we get close, I read the man's name tag: Dr. Russo, and then under that, Summerdale Veterinary Center. He must be the vet Kayla raves about. She loves his way with her pets and thinks the animal shelter he started in a state-of-the-art building behind his office is also amazing. That's where she got Simba. She said Dr. Russo also works closely with Best Friends Care, matching shelter dogs to military veterans in need of a therapy dog.

"Hi, I'm Dominic, leader of this band of beasts," he says with a charming smile. He inclines his head toward the dog he's holding. "This is PJ. All of these animals are available for adoption. Let me know if you'd like to get to know one, and I'll take them out for you."

"Can we pet PJ?" Grace asks.

Dr. Russo crouches down, turning so they can see the dog's face better. If a dog could look haughty and annoyed, this one does. "Real gentle," Dr. Russo says. "He's not used to kids."

The girls do a great job petting him gently. Grace runs two

fingers across his square head. Amelia pets around the back of his ear, and the dog's pointy ear twitches.

"PJ's a senior citizen dog, thirteen years old," Dr. Russo says.

"Thirteen isn't old," Grace says. "Twenty is old."

"It is for a dog," Dr. Russo says.

The girls rush to their mom. "Can we keep him?" Grace asks.

"Yeah!" Amelia says.

Izzy shakes her head. "We've talked about this. No pets until you're old enough to take responsibility for it yourselves."

"I can!" Grace exclaims.

"Me too!" Amelia says.

Izzy shakes her head.

Dr. Russo straightens to his full height and leans back to check in with PJ, who still looks annoyed. Or maybe that's just his squashed-in face and tired-looking big eyes. This dog needs a mellower home than the girls' house. They'd probably dress him up like a doll and push him around in a carriage. The indignity!

The girls dash off to look at a pair of cats. Izzy pets PJ, speaking softly to him.

"Thinking about getting a dog?" a familiar baritone voice asks from behind me.

A hot shiver runs down my spine as I turn to face Levi. "Just visiting with the girls."

He kisses my cheek. "Glad I tracked you down again. I'm done my official duties."

"Hey, Levi," Dr. Russo says. "Another beagle came in. I was hoping to run into you here. She's up to date with shots, spayed, and looking for a good home." He lowers his voice. "Sadie was abandoned because she barked too much when her owner was at work. She couldn't handle the long hours alone in an apartment, and it was disturbing the neighbors. I think she'd do best in a two-dog household."

Levi groans. "Baxter is already a handful." He softens. "Where is she?"

Dr. Russo sets PJ down, who immediately looks up at him expectantly. Dr. Russo pulls a treat from his pocket and gives it to him before putting him back in a crate with a soft bed.

A moment later, Dr. Russo brings out a beagle with similar markings to Baxter. Sadie's are black, tan, white and red. Baxter has more brown than red. She's beautiful and goes straight to Levi, sniffing his leg like it's the most interesting scent in the world.

Levi crouches down to pet her. "She probably smells Baxter." Sadie jumps on him, licking his face. Levi chuckles, pushing her back down and petting her behind the ears. She closes her eyes in pure bliss. Yeah, I know that feeling from those magical fingers. Ahem.

"She's two," Dr. Russo says. "And that's all I'm going to say about that."

Levi looks up at him. "Is she an escape artist?"

"Not that I heard."

Levi looks at Sadie. "Should I take you? Would you like a doggy friend?"

Sadie jumps on him, her paws against his shoulders as she licks his ear.

Levi smiles. "I think that's a yes. I'll take her."

My heart squeezes. This is a man with a lot of love to give. I can feel my defenses crumbling as he takes Sadie's leash and pets her while signing paperwork at the same time.

Heart of gold. It's tough to stay mad at him for springing a lawyer on me and escalating the battle with Kevin when I see him in action like this. He's a good person with good intentions. I think he was genuinely trying to help me, even though I would've much preferred advance notice and a private meeting.

Izzy and the girls join him and go crazy for Sadie, who runs circles around the girls, getting them tangled in her leash.

"What's her name?" Grace asks.

"Sadie," Levi says.

"You're so lucky! Mom won't let us get *anything*."

"When you're older," Izzy says.

"Can we visit Sadie at your house?" Grace asks.

"If it's okay with your mom, sure," Levi says. "But not today. I need to get her settled in with her new roommate, my other beagle Baxter."

"Two dogs!" Grace exclaims.

The girls turn pleading looks at their mom.

"When you're the mayor, you can get two dogs too," I tell the girls.

"What's a mayor do?" Grace asks.

Levi crouches down to explain his job while untangling Sadie's leash from the girls and petting her at the same time. Forget butterflies dancing in my stomach, now my ovaries are dancing.

Izzy sends me a knowing look.

It might be time to take a chance on love. A shiver goes through me at the thought.

No holding back! The new Galena takes risks. If only it weren't so scary.

15

Levi

I was so busy with town responsibilities and getting Sadie settled with Baxter, I only briefly saw Galena with her family at the fair. But now I'm heading next door to a barbecue at Kayla and Adam's house. Kayla said she invited Galena, so I'm hoping she's here.

I spot her right away in a circle of women gathered around a baby in a stroller. It's Sydney's daughter, Quinn. Galena's nieces are talking animatedly to the baby and offering her a rattle that she keeps throwing.

"Hey, everyone," I say and then give Galena a kiss on the cheek.

She blushes, looking up at me. "Hey, stranger. Kevin is seriously pissed about the lawyer. He keeps sending me angry texts from work."

I tuck a lock of hair behind her ear. "He's mad because he finally realized he has to give up the idea of the two of you getting together."

"That's what I said!" Izzy says.

The women gathered around baby Quinn agree. It's the usual crowd from ladies' night.

"I'm happy to offer my real-estate expertise," Paige says.

She used to work in real estate in the city. "And I can help stage your house for a fast sale."

"Lawyer proceedings can move slowly," I warn.

"Summer is the best time to sell, though," Paige says.

Galena rubs her temple. "I'd really like to not think about the Kevin situation for a while."

I rub her back. "Just trying to make the Kevin problem go away."

"What do you need fixed?" a woman barks from behind us. "I've got the answer or know someone who does."

We all turn to see Mrs. Joan Ellis, aka General Joan. We may all be biased with the general stuff because she was our third-grade teacher, and we were all a little scared of her.

"Hi, Mrs. Ellis," we all say in a motley chorus.

"How's everyone doing?" she asks, her sharp eyes taking in each of us by turn.

Everyone answers fine, but Mrs. Ellis barely notices, her eyes glued to Galena. "Glad to see you have the good sense to stick with Levi. So why do you look so miserable? Did Levi do something wrong? Just tell him what the problem is, and I'm sure he'll apologize." She sends me a hard look.

"Oh, it's not him who's the problem," Galena says.

Kayla, the oversharer, immediately tells Mrs. Ellis the entire situation in detail from the awful wedding disaster to the shared house in need of selling.

General Joan turns to me. "Remember how we talked about Harper filming in town? Let's make it happen. She's working on a thriller at the moment. We'll get them to film at Galena's house, and then Harper will convince Kevin to sell. If he's not already a fanboy, we can entice him with the glamour of being an extra in a scene. You'd be amazed at how being close to the film action can affect a person."

"How exactly will Harper convince him to sell?" Galena asks.

"She's very influential," the General says simply.

"It couldn't hurt," I say.

General Joan lifts a finger. "And the production company

will pay you for the use of your house for a few days. I'm sure we could find someone to take the two of you in, separately, of course, during filming."

Sydney pipes up, "Let's make it happen, Mrs. Ellis. I haven't seen Harper in forever, and I want Caroline and Quinn to meet."

"Caroline is two now and becoming a handful," General Joan warns. "I'm not sure how well behaved she'll be with an infant."

"Quinn's tough."

We all look at the four-month-old in her stroller just as she hurls her rattle for Grace and Amelia to fetch.

"Maybe she'll do okay," General Joan allows.

Everyone laughs.

~

Galena

After my sister and nieces go home, I go next door with Levi to his place. We're not here to talk. I hope.

The moment the door shuts behind us, his mouth crashes over mine. I love it. All my problems, all my worries, fade into nothing. This works, and I'm done questioning it.

Next thing I know, we're tearing at each other's clothes right there in the front entryway. He hits the light switch off and then lifts me, balanced against the door. It's hard and fast and exactly what I need. This big man pounding into me, his strong arms supporting me, the muscles in his back flexing under my palms. He slides a hand between us, stroking me, and I go off. His mouth swallows my harsh cry, and then he lets go.

I cling to him in the aftermath, panting. He kisses me, framing my face with his hands. And then he turns on the light and helps me get dressed. There's something so intimate about him dressing me, his gaze taking me in, his hands gentle as he smooths my shirt into place.

We smile at each other.

He cradles my jaw and kisses me gently. "I have to go back to the lake tonight for the fireworks for a ceremony I preside over. We could watch them together."

"I'd like that." I pull his head down and kiss him again.

A long while later, he lifts his head. "Your sister told me—"

I pull away. "Izzy talked to you about me?"

"Yeah, when you were supervising your nieces playing with Tank and Simba at Kayla's house. She told me your ex did some damage, and you need more time to be ready for a relationship. It's hard for me to wait, but you take whatever time you need, even if that means not seeing me for a little while." He gazes into my eyes with such warmth, my limbs go weak. "Okay? I just want you to be comfortable."

"Do you want a relationship?"

"I do," he says solemnly.

A shiver runs down my spine. "That sounded like a wedding vow."

"I'm open to the whole tamale."

"What's the whole tamale?"

"Marriage, kids, the works. No rush, but I want to experience that."

"Do you still feel like you're running out of time and have to cram in a lot of new experiences because you're getting closer to your dad's age when he died?"

He wraps an arm around my waist and pulls me close. "Funny. Since I met you, time seemed to stop. It's a different headspace. The Galena space."

My heart pounds. I could love this man. I do love this man. And then his large hand cups my jaw, and his lips meet mine in a tender kiss.

"I could use some water," he says, lightening the mood. "How about you?"

"Sure."

I follow him to the kitchen. He opens the refrigerator for the filtered pitcher and then shuts the door, looking worried. "Have you seen Baxter and Sadie? I just realized they didn't rush me at the front door. And Baxter usually comes in here every time I open the fridge."

"No, I haven't seen them."

He sets the pitcher on the table and shouts, "Baxter, come! Sadie?"

No dogs appear.

Levi sends me an alarmed look and checks the entire downstairs and then peers into the backyard. "Baxter's an escape artist. Climbing fences, digging under them, but I kept him inside when I went next door."

"Is he afraid of fireworks? Maybe he's hiding. I heard people setting them off earlier."

He lifts his brows and rushes to the living room. He crouches down, looking under the sofa. "There you are!"

I join him. *Aww.* Poor Baxter is lying nearly flat between the wall and the sofa. Sadie's next to him, looking calm like she's just keeping him company. Neither of them moved with all the activity in the front hall. *Thankfully.*

Levi gestures to Baxter. "I thought you'd escaped on me again. Come on out. You too, Sadie."

Baxter doesn't move, so Sadie doesn't either.

I get an idea. "Ooh, I know! Put a biscuit on the floor in front of the sofa. Then when he's ready to face the world, he'll have some incentive. I think it's Baxter who got scared, and she's just being his support buddy."

Levi goes to the kitchen and returns with a box of biscuits. He gives it a shake and calls for Baxter again. There's a snuffling noise, but no movement.

Levi breaks up a large biscuit in pieces and leaves a trail from the sofa to Baxter's dog bed next to the sofa. "Maybe we'll find him there later."

I smile. Levi deserves everything good in this world. I hope I can give him that.

A short while later, we leave hand in hand to go to the fireworks by the lake, leaving the dogs behind with Levi's T-shirt to keep them company. It sorta feels like we're a little family. For the first time in forever, I'm excited about the future. Not just content but *excited*. I never thought being a jilted bride could bring me so much happiness.

Only one person could ruin this, and I refuse to think about him. Tonight everything's perfect.

~

Two weeks later…

Kevin and I are in a standoff. Actually, he's standing still, like an ostrich with his head in the sand. He hasn't gotten a lawyer. In fact, he told me he forgave me for cheating on him and wants everything to go back to normal. What a joke.

My lawyer says I'm entitled to sixty percent of the value of the house because I put in sixty percent of the money toward buying it. We've only lived here a few months, so haven't spent anything on improvements. In any case, Kevin won't sell. He's dug his heels in, thinking if we just keep living together long enough, eventually I'll forgive him for calling off the wedding the way he forgave me for cheating. That's his frequent moral high ground. Except I never cheated!

Levi has given me space, so I don't feel pressured into a relationship, and he's also been tolerant of the fact that I still live with my ex. He grumbles about it, but so far it hasn't made him want to stop seeing me. I never spend the night at Levi's house. I don't want Kevin to have the house to himself for long stretches and think I'm giving up the house.

Tonight's a rare Friday night when Kevin and I are both home on time from work. Whenever I see him at home, he's irritable, yet still occasionally tosses out the possibility of a reconciliation. I'm eating spaghetti at the kitchen table, and he's sitting on the counter, eating a leftover sub sandwich, the carton of milk next to him. Honestly, I can't believe how stubborn he's being, which is what I tell him.

"I know one day you'll forgive me the way I forgave you," he says. "Then we can move on." He chugs milk straight from the carton.

"Could you get a glass for the milk? I use that milk in my cereal."

"It's almost gone," he says, taking another long swallow.

Maybe I should start putting my name on the food I buy.

I put my fork down. "Look, all I want is to sell this place and move on with my life."

He lifts his palms. "This *is* your life."

I clench my teeth, even though I want to scream that it's over, and I never, ever want to be with him again.

"I still love you," he says around a mouthful of sandwich. He pushes lettuce back into his mouth. *Gross.* "I told you I just got cold feet."

"Kevin, I don't love you anymore. Wouldn't you be happier moving on? You could meet someone new."

"I don't want someone new. I want you. You couldn't find two more compatible people if a computer matched us up. Oh, wait. It did." We met through a dating app.

"People are more complex than what any dating profile can match."

He finishes his sandwich, drains the milk, and crumples the carton. "You need to cut Levi out of your life. I don't appreciate you flaunting the guy you cheated on me with in front of me."

I push back from the table and stand, my appetite gone. "I never cheated on you, and I don't flaunt Levi!"

"He's always showing up here, constantly texting you and calling. You think I don't notice? You get this stupid look on your face when you hear from him."

I speak through my teeth. "I seriously can't stand to look at you anymore, let alone talk to you."

"That's Levi talking."

"It's not Levi! It's me."

The doorbell rings, and I hear Baxter's *arroo* dog yodel. Sadie joins in with cheerful barks. They're reacting to the doorbell Levi just rang.

"There's the cause of all our problems," Kevin says.

I go to the door. "Hey, Levi, now's not a great time."

Baxter sniffs the porch steps for interesting scents. Sadie nudges my hand for pets.

Kevin appears by my side and puts an arm around my shoulders. I shrug him off. "We were just talking about you."

Levi bristles. "Is there a problem?"

"Yeah, you," Kevin says. "I suggest you step out of this picture. You don't belong."

I shake my head. "Sorry. He keeps insisting you and I were together behind his back. I don't want you to be sucked into this."

Levi steps into the house and jabs Kevin in the chest. "Your lies won't get you what you want, and you gave up all rights to Galena when you dumped her on her wedding day."

"It was cold feet!" Kevin exclaims. "Why doesn't anyone believe me? Besides, I said no to the wedding, not Galena. As far as I'm concerned, we never broke up."

"Kevin, we did break up," I say, completely exasperated with the man.

"Galena and I had a great time in Vegas," Levi says smugly.

Levi and Kevin stare each other down, the tension high. I really hope they're not going to fight. First because I don't want anyone getting hurt, and second, because I'm afraid Kevin will have all kinds of ammunition for a lawyer one day.

I appeal to Kevin's reasonable side, if it's still in there. "Kevin, Levi was there for me on our wedding day after you dumped me, and I invited him to join me in Vegas on the spur of the moment. There was no relationship before that. I'm not a cheater."

"I'm not stupid," he snaps. "I'm willing to put it behind us, but he has to go."

"Galena, could we take a walk?" Levi asks, his expression grim. "We need to talk."

My senses go on full alert. That sounds ominous.

"Sounds like a breakup talk," Kevin says with a smug

smile. "Go ahead, Galena. I'll be waiting here for you when you get back."

I step outside with Levi and take a deep breath of fresh air. Sometimes it feels like Kevin sucks all the air out of the room.

Levi's quiet as we walk to the lake.

"Sorry about that," I say. "Kevin's being stubborn."

"It's more than that. He still loves you."

"I know he says that, but he really loves the way I used to love him. Our relationship centered around him. I'm not doing that anymore."

He stops at the end of our street, the lake shining in the distance. Baxter pulls toward the lake, and I wish I could go too. Levi looks way too serious, and I'm getting a bad feeling about what he's going to say. My eyes get hot. It's the breakup talk, I know it. "Galena—"

"You said you'd give me time to know if I'm ready for more. It's only been two weeks."

He scrubs a hand over his face. "I've tried to give you space, I really have, but it's hard when I know you're still with *him*."

"But I'm not with him."

"I'm sick of always dropping you off at home with him! I need to know that you're okay at home, not wonder how it's going."

"I told you I'm fine."

"Well, I'm not. I hate this."

"You hate being with me?" I ask softly.

He looks off in the distance. "This is hard for me to say…"

"Then don't."

His eyes are intent on mine. "I love you, but I can't do this anymore. Not until you separate from Kevin permanently."

My eyes sting, my throat tight, and that just makes me furious. "This is why I wasn't ready for a relationship. You're hurting an already hurting heart. You said you wouldn't push me, yet here you are two weeks later pushing."

He gives me a sympathetic look that makes me want to bawl. "I'm not pushing. I'm stepping out of the picture. I'm not helping anything, and I don't want to be between you two anymore. As long as he's in your life, I'm not. It's as simple as that."

"My life is complicated. I know that, but—"

He kisses my cheek. "Bye, Galena."

And then he strides toward the lake, his faithful dogs trotting happily by his side. I watch them until they're just specks in the distance. Finally, I turn and trudge toward home.

And then I can't face Kevin, so I get in my car and drive to my sister's place. She'll know what to do.

Only she doesn't. Because as she says, *you're caught between two men, and men don't share.*

Hell, I don't want to share either. I just want my house back and Levi. Not necessarily in that order.

16

Levi

It's been a week, and I can barely sleep at night, thoughts of Galena tumbling through my mind. The way her face lights up with her smile, her quick wit, even her glasses magnifying her deep brown eyes. And those sexy nights we shared. Just all of her. But what was I supposed to do, keep taking her out and bringing her home to *him*, the smug prick who was trying to paint me as the villain? And I never knew if she was okay. It was everything a responsible person would never do— leave a loved one in a dicey domestic situation. I couldn't take it anymore.

I stare at my laptop at work in town hall, trying to focus on my many responsibilities. The town clerk, Megan, a woman in her fifties with blond and white hair, walks in with a cheerful smile. "Mail call!"

"Just set it in the basket."

She pulls out a large cardboard mailer that has DO NOT BEND written on it in black marker in several places. "Looks like photos. Did you get new mayor photos on vacation?"

"No." I look at the return address. It's from Galena's grandmother. "It's personal."

"Ooh, personal."

I give her a pointed look. She grins and walks back to her desk by reception.

I rip open the mailer and pull out photos with a note written on pink paper. Our fake wedding reception photos. My gut lurches with just a quick glance at our smiling faces. I read the note:

Levi,
Now this looks like a whirlwind romance if I've ever seen it. Don't give up on our Galena. She's worth it.

Hope to see you again soon!
Betsy

I blow out a breath and go through the pictures. Galena and I standing close together by the gift table, feeding each other cake, the kiss-the-bride moment, and the moment after that where we're gazing into each other's eyes with equal looks of shock and wonder.

I rub my temple. Galena must've told her grandparents we broke up. I convinced myself that Galena didn't have room for me in her life, that she didn't love me the way I did her, but now, looking at these photos, I see that what we had was there right from the start. She looks as into me as I do her. And that was day one. We've only gotten closer since then.

The real problem is Kevin. Not me and Galena.

I spend the next hour coming up with a plan based on General Joan's genius idea to get Harper to film here. I'd forgotten about it while I was so focused on keeping Galena close to me. If you don't like the situation you're stuck in, change it. Least that's how I always operate. I can't make Kevin leave that house, I can't make Galena leave that house, but maybe Harper can.

By the next day, the plan is in motion. I called for an emergency meeting last night and got the town council to sign off on letting our hometown actor Harper Ellis film here through Claire Jordan's production company. Claire Jordan is an A-list movie star. Harper works with her regularly. That was the easy part, and it wasn't that easy either. Now I need to convince Harper to film at Galena's house so Galena and Kevin will have to leave it. If I can't get Galena out of a tense domestic situation, maybe a famous actor can. Galena's lawyer is taking too long.

I head to The Horseman Inn to meet with Mrs. Ellis, aka General Joan, for lunch. She said she wanted to talk to me about Harper's film. I'm hoping she has the inside scoop I can use when I talk to Harper.

I'm surprised to find General Joan in the back dining room sitting with Harper, who looks radiant, her skin glowing, her curly hair full and glossy. I swear she gets more beautiful with age. Did I mention I once took her to the eighth-grade dance? My claim to fame. It's kinda cool I knew her back in the day.

Harper stands and opens her arms to me, her snug yellow T-shirt clinging to a slightly rounded belly. I don't remember that last time. Pregnancy or weight gain? I keep my mouth shut. "Surprise!"

I hug her. "This is a surprise. We just got clearance for filming, and here you are. Mrs. Ellis, you didn't say a word."

The General points to a chair. "Sit. I didn't know. Harper showed up unannounced for her big news." Then she beams a rare smile at Harper, her eyes shiny with unshed tears.

Harper leans close to my ear to whisper, "I'm pregnant. Keep it quiet, okay? Just three months along."

"It could be twins," the General whisper-shouts. "Look how big she is already."

"Thanks, Grandmom," Harper says drily. "It's not twins. I just popped out faster this time. I'm afraid it's not all baby in my belly. I've been eating a lot of bread. Too many carbs."

"There's nothing wrong with bread," the General huffs.

"What's next, milk? Can we please leave the basics alone? If the baby wants you to eat more bread, then that's exactly what you should do. Are you taking your prenatal vitamins?"

"Yes, and please keep your voice down," Harper says. "We don't want it to be public yet."

"I am keeping my voice down. I was just talking about bread and vitamins."

Harper and I exchange an amused look.

"Anyway," Harper says to me, "I heard there's a specific house you had in mind for filming. Think we could take a look at it today?"

"I could show you the outside. Let me text the owner to see if she could show you the inside. She's at work." *And I haven't told her about my plan yet.* I text Galena while the General whispers urgent questions to Harper about her pregnancy.

Me: *Hey, do you remember Harper Ellis? She's in town scouting for a location for her movie. I suggested your house because it has that great patio and second-story deck. Any chance you can come home on your lunch break and show her the interior?*

Galena: *Why my house?*

Me: *Because of that deck and patio.*

No response. *Shit.* This isn't going well, and Harper's here. I need to convince Harper before she sees other properties.

Me: *The production company would pay for the use of the property. It could go toward your lawyer bills and settle this thing for good.*

Galena: *It sounds like an inconvenience. I'd have to get Kevin to agree, he probably won't, and why don't I hear from you for an entire week and now you talk like everything's normal. You broke up with me, remember?*

My gut does a slow roll. I should've brought up this possibility yesterday, but there were so many things that had to fall into place, I wasn't sure if it would happen. Now it's all coming together quickly.

Me: *It's hard to explain by text. I miss you. I'm trying to help us move forward together.*

Galena: …

I hold my breath. The dots disappear. My stomach drops. She's not going to answer; she's done with me. I swallow over a lump of emotion and look at the expectant faces of Harper and the General.

"Uh, I might have to…" I trail off as my phone dings with another text.

Galena: *I'll check with Kevin. Earliest I can get there would be five thirty.*

I let out a long breath. "She says she has to check with the guy who lives with her. Earliest will be five thirty."

"You'll stay for dinner," the General tells Harper.

"But I'll miss Caroline's bath time."

The General calmly pulls her phone from her purse and taps a few times. "Hello, Garrett. It's Grandmom." That's Harper's husband. General Joan titters, rolling her eyes. "I'm not a queen; stop that foolishness." She smiles widely and then continues. "Harper insists on staying for dinner here with me, so I'll need you to join us with Caroline. Harper doesn't want to miss her bath time. You can all spend the night with me if you like."

Harper shakes her head and whispers to me, "He'll do anything for her."

"No, you don't need to bring your toolbox," the General says. "Everything is in good repair thanks to you. Just bring yourself and my sweet girl." She giggles—actually giggles— and smooths her hair. "Fresh. We'll see you soon." She turns to Harper. "He says I'm his sweet girl. That man sure knows how to flatter a woman."

"You have him wrapped around your little finger," Harper says.

General Joan waves that away. "Nonsense."

Harper takes a drink of water. "So, where were we?"

"Could you tell me more about your movie?" I ask.

Harper's eyes sparkle with excitement. "It's a domestic

thriller set partly in a suburban house, and then it goes to a cat-and-mouse chase in the city. I'm playing the woman on the hunt after I turn the tables on my seemingly innocent husband."

"How're you going to hide your pregnancy on camera?" the General asks.

Harper glances around at a few people eating lunch looking over curiously. "It's still a secret."

"Not to the camera," the General points out.

"I'll hold stuff in front of my belly or wear something loose. We're going to make it work."

The General wags her finger. "No stunts."

"No stunts," Harper agrees. "There's a double for that."

The waiter arrives to take our order. Harper fills me in on the film schedule and the number of crew likely to be needed for the Summerdale part of filming. It's all fascinating to me. I had no idea it took so many people to film even just a small segment of a movie.

My phone vibrates with a text.

Galena: *Kevin is excited. I didn't realize he was such a big Harper fan. He'll be at the house in an hour. I'd better go too, since we both need to sign off on stuff. I'll have to work late tonight to make up the time.*

Me: *Awesome. I think this will be good for everyone involved. I'll see you soon.*

Galena: *Is this going to be awkward? You, me, Kevin.*

Me: *And Harper. It'll be fine.*

I fill Harper in on the latest. A moment later, lunch arrives, and we dig in. The General is a slow eater. Harper and I finish our meals just as a chorus of female voices calls out to her.

"Oh my God, it's Harper Ellis!" Sydney exclaims, throwing her hands in the air.

"I'm such a fan!" Jenna says, patting a hand over her heart.

"Me too!" Audrey says, smiling.

The original four, joined at the hip since the first grade, reunite in a happy group hug. I grew up with them. Everyone eventually came back to town except Harper. Sydney owns this place, Jenna runs Summerdale Sweets, and Audrey is our town librarian.

Harper exclaims over Jenna's pregnant belly. "Look at you! When are you due?"

Jenna rubs her belly. "September twenty-third."

"Can't wait to meet baby Robinson!" Harper says. "And how's your baby Robinson?" she asks Sydney.

Sydney inclines her head. "She's a Winters with the Robinson fire. Wyatt's doing the pacing-back-and-forth thing, trying to get her to nap. She'd much rather stay awake all day until she collapses at night in a wretched crying heap. She's a fighter."

"Of sleep," I say.

Everyone laughs.

"And how's your book baby?" Harper asks Audrey kindly, trying to include her in all the baby stuff.

Audrey waves that away. "Not the same, but yeah, uh, I finished it." She stares at Harper's stomach. "Wait, are you…"

"Yup!"

"Oh my God, congratulations!"

A slew of congratulations and hugs follows before the General barks, "Sit down, all of you. Have some decorum. This is a nice restaurant."

"Why, thank you, Mrs. Ellis," Sydney says. "Since it's my restaurant, our behavior is tolerated just fine."

The General harrumphs and then turns to Audrey. "I could help you on the man front, you know."

We all stifle a laugh. Here comes Cupid.

Audrey's hand goes to her throat. "I don't need help, but thank you anyway."

The General hitches a thumb at me. "You missed your chance with this guy. His heart's taken."

Harper turns to me. "Ooh, are you still with that cute brunette with the glasses? The one I took a picture with last time I was in town?"

"Galena, well, not exactly together at the moment. I'm working on it."

The General pats my shoulder. "I have complete confidence in you." Then she turns her sharp gaze on Audrey. "You're next."

"Next for what?" Harper asks.

"Your grandmother believes she's our town Cupid," I say.

"I *am* the town Cupid," the General says. "I've lost count of how many couples I helped get together, including helping you ladies. Don't deny it!" She points at the group in one slow gesture across them before stopping her pointing finger at Audrey. All the women become still and silent. Retired third-grade teacher still has the magic touch.

Audrey laughs nervously and twirls her long dark hair. "Actually, I'm going out with someone new tomorrow night. Turns out he's a veteran, so he was interested in hearing more about my book research into military history."

Her friends erupt with a chorus of questions.

"Who?"

"For real?"

"What are you wearing?"

"It's really not a big deal." Audrey turns to me. "I heard there's going to be filming in town. I'm happy to offer the library as a location."

The women burst out laughing.

"What?" Audrey asks, offended. "It could be romantic or suspenseful among the shelves."

"It's a thriller," Harper says. "I don't think it would work. Thanks, though."

Jenna gives Audrey a sly smile. "So tell us about your fake date, Aud."

Audrey twirls her hair again, looking guilty. "It's not fake."

"We know your tells," Sydney says, twirling her auburn hair and looking guilty.

Audrey drops her hair. "It's Dr. Russo, okay? He was very nice to me when I took Cinder in for another checkup. She's been losing weight, and we don't know why. She's on a special diet with vitamin injections, so we've been seeing each other weekly because of it." Cinder is her gray cat. She used to have a white cat named Ella, but she got loose and never came back. Years ago, I helped her put signs up all over town for help in recovering Ella.

Jenna's brows lift. "Interesting. How did he ask you out? Was it like, how's Cinder, and let's get a drink on Saturday?"

Audrey shakes her head. "Not quite." She looks to the ceiling for a moment before saying in a rush, "He said are you busy on Saturday night, and I said no, and he said let's get a drink. We're meeting in Clover Park at the Happy Endings bar."

"How did you know he was a veteran?" Sydney asks, still sounding suspicious.

The General arches a brow at me in question. I don't know if Audrey's telling the truth. Who could blame her for wanting to push the General's matchmaking attention away from her?

Audrey speaks slowly, like she's thinking at the same time. "Well, uh, we talked about my book and how Best Friends Care helps veterans, and why Dr. Russo supports the cause. He was medically discharged from the Marines after he busted his leg up. It's better now, but he's not in fighting condition. Then he went to veterinary school, and now here he is."

"That actually sounds true," Sydney says.

Audrey twirls her hair and then drops it. "Mmm-hmm, we talk."

"You still call him Dr. Russo?" Harper asks. "I call him Dominic."

"He earned a degree," Audrey half mumbles, looking away.

"Wow, go, Audrey!" Jenna lifts a hand for a high five and has to wait a long moment for Audrey to return it. "He's a great guy. I work with him a lot in support of the animal shelter. That's where I got my awesome dog Mocha."

"Agree," Harper says. "I've spoken with him several times on behalf of Best Friends Care."

Sydney's lips twist to the side. "Then why not meet here, Aud? You had all your other first dates here so we could check them out for you."

Audrey grabs my water, takes a big gulp, and then coughs, choking on water.

I pat her back. "Are you okay?"

Drew Robinson appears out of nowhere. "Are you choking?"

Audrey's face is bright red as she waves him away, her eyes tearing. "I'm fine. Just went down the wrong pipe."

"What're you doing here, big bro?" Sydney asks him in a teasing voice.

Drew's gaze remains on Audrey, watching to be sure she's okay. "I was looking for Audrey. She wasn't at the library."

"You know she's allowed to leave the library, right?" Jenna asks. She likes to give Drew a hard time because he never does anything about his attraction to Audrey. It's hard to say if it's lust or deep concern, but he's often where she's at, checking to be sure she's all right.

"Now here's a real man," the General announces, giving Drew a sly look even as she praises him. "A veteran who owns his own business. Old enough to settle down." She turns to Drew. "I'd set you up with Audrey if she didn't already have a date with those very same qualifications tomorrow night."

Drew stares at Audrey. "You have a date with a guy like me?"

Audrey flushes and tucks her hair behind her ears. "Not exactly like you. It's no big deal. Anyway, Harper's pregnant."

He glances at Harper. "Congratulations." He turns back to Audrey. "Who's the guy?"

"Dr. Russo," she says hoarsely and then clears her throat. "Dominic, I mean."

Drew crosses his arms. "I just stopped by to tell you about

a new Eisenhower biography. Thought you might be interested in it since you've gotten into military history."

"Thank you," she says. "Just leave the information at the front desk, and I'll see if we can order it."

The women all stare at him expectantly.

Finally, he grumbles, "Sure. I gotta get back to work."

"Bye!" the women chorus, except Audrey, who's back to twirling her hair and looking guilty for some reason.

Drew strides toward the door. There's barely a hitch in his step when the General says loudly, "Drew, you're next on my Cupid list!"

17

———

Galena

Okay, this is surreal. *The* Harper Ellis, whom I fangirled over the first time I met her, is now at my house, and I'm giving her a tour! Levi is here too, and I was afraid that was going to be a problem with Kevin, but Kevin is so enthralled with Harper he's speechless as he trails along with us. He keeps sneaking looks at her.

We finish the tour back in the living room.

"You have a beautiful home," Harper says.

"Thank you," I say, sounding slightly out of breath. I love this house, a white with black shutters colonial built in the seventies. It's exactly the four-bedroom, two-and-a-half bath with a backyard place that I dreamed of as a kid. The kind of house a family can spread out in instead of living on top of each other like my family did in our apartment. Though I'm missing the family part of it. No kids, no husband.

"You can film here as long as you want," Kevin blurts. "I'll crash on my friend's couch."

My jaw drops. He'll move for Harper, but not for me? "I'm okay with you filming here too. I can stay elsewhere as needed."

Kevin nods like a bobblehead doll.

Levi gives me a slow, sexy smile behind Kevin's back.

Heat rushes through my body. He probably thinks I'll be staying with him. We haven't talked about getting back together, but I'm starting to get the idea that this whole thing is his plan to make that happen in a way he can deal with. I've had some time to think about it, and I probably wouldn't like him living with an ex either.

Harper scans the downstairs again, looking deep in thought. "Okay, I'm going to show the pictures I took to my producer, Claire, but I think it's a go. It helps that it's almost a blank slate. You didn't paint or decorate much at all. Now our set designer can easily make it whatever we need. Would it be okay with you if we gave the kitchen a makeover? Update the cabinets, counters, and sink to make it look more contemporary? The appliances already look new, so they're good as is."

"No problem," Kevin says.

"Sounds good to me," I say.

Harper smiles. "Great. You'll be paid for the use of your home. I'll send over the paperwork once I get the okay from Claire. Oh, I should've mentioned filming starts in a month, and it'll take two weeks. Does that work?"

"Yes," Kevin and I say in near unison.

"Can I get you a drink?" Kevin asks Harper.

"I'd love some water."

He goes into the kitchen with her.

I turn to Levi and whisper, "I had no idea Kevin was such a fanboy of Harper's. I swear if she said jump off a cliff, he'd do it."

"She's very popular. I'm not surprised." He pulls me close and whispers in my ear, "This is me winning you back without Kevin in the picture. He's the problem, not us."

"I'm glad to hear you say that. Totally agree."

"Move in with me."

My breath hitches. Living together isn't a step I take lightly. "Just for two weeks of filming."

He kisses my temple. "For now."

∾

Levi

When I set up the film deal, I mostly did it to get Galena away from Kevin and give us a chance. Of course, it's great for the town too. Over the past month, I've kept seeing Galena tiptoeing around her ex because if I see the guy, there's going to be another confrontation, which helps no one. It's been tough for me, but worth it because Galena has opened up to me little by little, week by week. Now that we're a week into filming, everything is great between us. She moved in with me last weekend.

Not only has it been awesome having Galena live with me, I've been spending a lot of time watching filming at her house when she's at work. It's really cool to see how the cast and crew work together to create a scene and tell a story. I've been questioning every crew member, asking about their job and the techniques that go into it.

Harper's been working her magic with Kevin, who's on set the entire time to watch. He took two weeks off work, which Galena says is unheard of for him. Anyway, I explained the situation with him to Harper, and she's going to let him have a little brush with fame. We're hoping if *she* tells him the best idea is to sell the house and move on, he'll actually listen. We'll see if a famous actor can change his mind. Reason didn't work, and I know exactly why. He's still in love with Galena. He never should've let her go in the first place. His loss and my gain.

I watch as a scene unfolds in the newly updated kitchen between Harper and her on-screen husband, Sam. Harper's playing a creepy character, who seems sweet and caring but has a dark side.

The director yells, "Cut! That's a wrap for today."

The crew puts away gear while the actors get out of the way.

Harper approaches me. "Want to be an extra in the barbecue party scene on the patio on Monday?"

"Sure. What do I need to do?"

"Just show up in a casual outfit and hold a drink in the background, pretending to talk to another extra."

"I can do that."

Kevin rushes over. "Great work today, Harper. It's incredible what you do. I read the script, and it seems so flat until you bring it to life."

"Thank you," she replies graciously. "Would you like to be an extra in the barbecue party scene on Monday?"

"Yes. Absolutely. What time?"

"Can you be here by eleven?"

"Definitely."

"No lines, but you'll be paid for your time. Ask Diana for the paperwork."

He makes a beeline for Diana.

I lean close to her ear. "Must be nice to have that kind of power. Men rush to do your bidding."

She inclines her head. "Some people are impressed when they meet someone they once saw on a big screen or their favorite TV show. Also, guys like him often confuse me with the characters I play. I peg him for the guy who loved my tough CEO character, which is the reason I hired Joe in the first place. Too many guys wanted to either bring her down a peg or have her be tough with them in a more intimate way." She catches her bodyguard's eye, Joe, who hovers nearby, looking menacing with his huge muscles and neck tattoo.

I lift a hand in greeting, and he jerks his chin.

"How're you going to get Kevin to sell?" I ask quietly.

She pulls my arm to get me closer, whispering back, "I'll tell him if it was on the market, I might be interested in buying it. This is my hometown."

I glance at her, surprised. "Really?"

"The point is to get it on the market. Anyone *might* buy it. Besides, I'm happy with our house in Brooklyn. I'm near Garrett's family, right across the street from his brother Sean and my sister-in-law Josie. She's my best friend and honorary sister. I'm happy to visit Grandmom frequently here, but, you know, a little distance makes the heart grow fonder, and our relationship warmer. She can be a little harsh sometimes."

"No, the General?"

She laughs. "Does *everyone* call her that behind her back? I thought it was just me and the girls."

"Word got around."

"Isn't it cute how she's turned matchmaker in her retirement?"

"Depends on if you're the one she's matchmaking."

She squeezes my arm. "I'm sure."

Kevin bounds over, his eyes huge. "It's a go. I'm going to be in your movie."

"Great!" Harper says brightly. "I'll get you tickets for the premiere in the city, so you can watch yourself on the big screen when it comes out."

Kevin's jaw drops, and he shuts it with a snap. "Really?"

"Absolutely. It's your house, and now you're part of the movie."

He glances at me. "Is everyone invited?"

"Limited availability," she says solemnly. "We always make a VIP list."

He runs both hands through his blond hair, his eyes wide. "Wow. Okay. Thank you so much."

"No problem. I need to get going." She waves to the crowd packing up. "Have a good weekend!" She gives me a hug goodbye and walks out the door, Joe right behind her.

"You're close with her, aren't you?" Kevin asks me.

"We grew up together." Then I can't help but brag a little. "I took her to the eighth-grade dance."

"Do you think she'll come through with tickets for the premiere?"

"Of course."

"Are you going?"

"I don't know if I'm invited."

"She didn't say anything to you?"

"Nope."

He rubs his hands on his jeans and lets out a shaky breath.

"Okay, okay. I need to figure out wardrobe for my scene. I can't believe this is really happening. Me in a movie, going to a premiere with Harper Ellis."

Before I can say he's invited to the premiere but not actually going with Harper, he dashes out the door, colliding with the boom operator. "Sorry!"

I help carry gear out to the van, talking to the crew as I do. The entire collaborative process of making a film enthralls me in the same way Kevin is enthralled by Harper. Now we can only hope her influence is enough to get him to do the right thing.

I made dinner in time for Galena's arrival at home. It's her favorite of my limited repertoire, spaghetti Bolognese made with homemade tomato sauce. Full confession: I buy the sauce at the local farmers' market. It still counts.

She walks in the door using her key, and Baxter races to the door, barking joyfully. His tail wags hard as he rushes her legs. Sadie runs to catch up a moment later, skidding to a stop in front of Galena. She crouches down to pet both of them. "There's my good boy. There's my good girl."

Baxter sniffs her ear and licks it, some of her hair getting caught on his nose.

She giggles and straightens. "It smells divine in here. Did you make my favorite?"

I close the distance and wrap my arms around her. "I did. How're you?"

She hugs me back. "I made good progress on the analysis of the latest data for the Alzheimer's drug. It's looking promising. How was filming?"

She walks into the kitchen, and I follow her, excited to share. "Really cool. I learned so much about the camera work and the angles they need for different scenes."

"You're really getting into the tech side, aren't you?"

"Not just the tech. The craft that each person brings to the table, from set design to props to lighting. Each person is an artist in their own right, and they work together to create their project, a story they share with the world."

She washes her hands and helps herself to a glass of water. "Ever think of becoming a filmmaker?"

I stare at her, stunned at the idea. "No. I never even considered it as a career, any part of it. It seemed like a faraway Hollywood thing."

"There's plenty of stuff filmed in New York too."

"That's what Harper said."

She smiles. "Something to consider."

I turn off the flame on the sauce, thinking about that. I have a responsibility toward Summerdale. This community stepped in for me and my family after Dad died. Serving as mayor is my way of paying back that debt. They always vote for me. Of course, no one else ever steps up for the position.

On the other hand, wasn't I all about being open to new experiences? That impending sense of doom has faded with Galena in my life. I haven't felt that urgency like I have to cram a lot in before I run out of time. Was it just love I was looking for to finally feel at peace?

What would happen if I dropped all my duties and responsibilities here and went back to school for filmmaking? Would Summerdale fall apart? Would I?

"Was Kevin there all day again?" Galena asks, snapping me out of my thoughts.

"As far as I know. He's going to be an extra on Monday, and he's giddy as a kid. Any interest in being an extra?"

"Me? No-o-o."

"Because you don't want to be around Kevin all day?"

"That, and I have no interest in being on camera. I shudder at the thought. In case you haven't noticed, I don't like being the center of attention. I'm quite content to work hard in the background, doing my thing."

"Then why did you agree to be in the magazine for your wedding?"

"As a favor to Kayla."

"Even though you shudder at the thought?"

She shrugs. "Doesn't matter now."

"He still has a thing for you."

She kisses me. "I've moved on."

I serve up dinner and set the plates on the table thinking about that. Now that she's living with me, I believe she's done with him. Yet part of me could never believe it while they lived together. What's going to happen when filming is over?

We eat dinner together, as we have for the past week. Baxter and Sadie park themselves under the table in case any crumbs fall. I could get used to this. She's so easy to be with, so easy to talk to, and her perspective on things is always unique. I tell her everything I learned today talking to the director of photography, who manages not just the cameras but also lighting, electrical, and grips. The director of photography is the leader of the camera crew and sets a scene as the director wants it to look.

We finish eating, and Galena clears the dishes, rinsing them and putting them in the dishwasher. We trade off like that. One cooks; the other cleans. I stand by her side at the sink, one thought niggling in the back of my mind.

"What?" she asks, glancing up at me.

"I didn't say anything."

"You're looking at me like you have something to say. What?"

"What if Kevin hadn't called off the wedding? You could be married to him right now."

"True." She closes the dishwasher and dries her hands on a towel. "I've thought a lot about this, and the thing is, I probably would've been content. We'd already lived together for two years, and we never fought. It would've been a safe, sane decision, but I hope at some point I would've realized there's more to a relationship than being compatible." She puts her arms around my neck and gives me a sexy smile.

Every nerve ending rises to attention and another choice part too. "Yeah?"

"Yeah. Like passion, excitement, enjoying doing stuff together instead of working all the time."

"Like pretending to be married at a wedding party?"

"Exactly."

"And playing slots in Vegas."

"Mmm…sometimes. And most importantly sharing chores." She smiles impishly. "Sharing is very important. A relationship should be a two-way street."

I put my hands on her hips and lift her to the counter. "Relationship, huh? That's where we're at now?"

"Finally, right? What took you so long to catch up?"

I kiss her and feel her smile against my lips. "So you're saying meeting me showed you there was another way to have a relationship." I step between her legs, pulling her close and kissing her long and deep. "A better way."

She kisses me passionately in response. Raw lust fires through me as I tangle my fingers in her hair and keep her close.

This one's mine. She has to be.

18

Galena

I took the day off to watch the last day of filming. It's a slow boring process, much slower than I thought to get through a scene. I find myself watching the two men in my life more than the actors. There's Levi, observing closely and talking to crew members whenever he can, and then there's Kevin, fixated on Harper. And the funny thing is, Levi and Kevin have been in the same house for two weeks now and barely spoken a word to each other, good or bad. It's like they're both too busy with the movie action to care.

I watch what I hope is the sixth and final take of the characters Lila and Sam saying goodbye as Sam goes off to work. He's suspicious of Lila at this point, but she has an explanation for everything. How their pet parrot died, where his favorite sweater went, why his parents canceled dinner on the same night she had a male coworker over for dinner. I haven't read the script, so I'm not sure where it's going. Levi says they're all clues about what Lila's up to and how she plans to kill Sam later to inherit his money. Levi says there's more wild twists after that, but I asked for no spoilers. I'll see it when it comes out next summer.

Finally, the director calls it a wrap, and everyone gets ready to go, packing up gear and talking cheerfully.

Kevin walks over to me, frowning. "I can't believe it's over so fast."

"It was two weeks. They're still filming in the city after this."

"I wonder if I can be an extra there too."

I stare at him. "How much time off work are you going to take?"

He stares at me like I'm the one acting strange. "Galena, I haven't taken a vacation day since I started at the lab four years ago. I've got the time, especially since I didn't go on the honeymoon in Vegas. Thank God. Now I can do this." *Yes, thank God.* He waves wildly. "Harper! Can I talk to you for a minute before you go?"

She smiles. "Sure. Just a minute while I finish up here."

"Harper and I talk every day," Kevin says to me. "She's getting me tickets to the premiere. I could ask if you want to go too."

"No, that's okay. You should ask a date."

He rubs his hands together, his normally cool demeanor bristling with energy. "Who wouldn't want to go to something cool like that?"

I'm surprised to hear him say it. "Right."

He meets my eyes. "Sorry. That was rude. You and I broke up not long ago, and we have a history. I shouldn't mention dating."

"Kevin, it's fine. I want you to be happy with someone else."

He checks if anyone's listening and then confides, "You're the only woman I've had a relationship with. I don't know if I'll ever find someone like you again."

I search for the words to gently tell him I've moved on, so he should too. "I appreciate you sharing that, but—"

"Hey, Harper!" he says with way too much enthusiasm as she appears in front of us.

I cringe. I hope I didn't sound like that much of a fan when I met her the first couple of times.

"I'm glad you're both here," Harper says. "You're both

invited to the film premiere, of course, and I'm going to Claire Jordan's film opening next weekend in the city, if you'd like tickets to that as well. I know it was an inconvenience for us to kick you out of your home. It's the least I can do."

Kevin gushes before I can get a word in. "I'll go! Thank you so much for your generosity."

"Thanks," I say. "I'll check with Levi. He's been really interested in the whole filmmaking process. He'd probably like to see it."

Harper smiles. "I noticed that too. I told him I could put him in touch with people who could point him in the right direction for film programs."

"That sounds exciting." I think of how Levi was so eager to try new things, and this sounds like a whole new world for him. But would that mean he leaves Summerdale?

"I'd love to watch you continue filming in the city," Kevin says to Harper. "I could be an extra there too. You wouldn't even have to pay me."

Harper and I both stare at Kevin. Her bodyguard crosses to stand next to Kevin, who looks up at him and swallows audibly.

"I'm not dangerous, I swear," Kevin says. "I've just never enjoyed myself more than being on set and being an extra. This is like a vacation to me."

Harper's smile remains in place, but her expression is guarded. "So glad you've been enjoying the experience. I'll have to get back to you on that."

"Of course. No problem. You have my card."

She takes us both in. "On a related note, I really like this house and wondered if you'd consider putting it on the market?"

"You want to buy our house?" Kevin asks incredulously. "You'd live in Summerdale?"

She lifts her palms. "I'm from here, after all. It's a possibility. Or I might know someone who'd be interested. A lot of my friends in the city are thinking of moving out to the suburbs for more space."

"Yes, absolutely," Kevin says. "Galena and I have been talking about selling, right, Galena?"

"Yes," I say immediately. More like I've been talking and he's been ignoring but whatever.

"Great!" Harper says brightly. "Let me know when it's on the market. And thank you both again for the use of your home."

"You're welcome," I say.

"My pleasure," Kevin says.

She smiles directly at me and then turns and walks out the door. Kevin collapses on the sofa, looking dazed.

The wardrobe lady, a pretty redhead in her thirties, flops down next to him. "So are we going to see you next week for filming?"

Kevin's eyes widen. "Yes. Would you like to go to the Claire Jordan premiere with me?"

"I'd love to."

I shift away, not quite sure where I should be at this moment. Kevin is finally moving on. His new friends will probably drop him once he goes back to work in the lab, but hey. Let him enjoy his time off.

Now what about me? Do I need to move back into the house to keep my claim on it, or should I stay with Levi until the house is sold? It's a lot to ask Levi to put up with me living with my ex, and Levi's place is comfortable. But am I just doing the easy thing jumping into another living-together situation with my boyfriend? Maybe it's best if I had some time living alone. My good mood tanks at the thought.

Kevin calls over to me, "Galena, this is Iris. She's a genius with wardrobe. This is my…friend Galena. We're roommates for now. I'll be getting my own place as soon as this one sells."

"I'm looking for a roommate," Iris says, putting her hand on his leg. "If you're going to be in the city."

He nods several times as he talks. "I work here, but I wouldn't mind crashing with you next week for filming and the premiere."

She offers her hand to shake. "Deal. You pay for groceries, and we'll call it even."

"I'll pay for more than that," he says magnanimously. "I'll look up Airbnb prices for the area and pay you the equivalent. This is my vacation. What's the address?"

She plays with the hair at the nape of his neck. "You are too cute. I might know another way we could trade for a fair deal."

He leaps from the sofa. "I'll pack my things."

She laughs. "Awesome."

Guess I'll be staying here by myself. Or maybe it's time to pack up my stuff, let Paige stage the house for a sale, and finally let go. I can stay with Levi until I can afford to buy my own place. What's the right thing to do? I'm so confused.

I let out a shaky breath. There might be something to what my parents said about not living together until we're married. Didn't I learn my lesson with Kevin? My heart races. Married? Is that even something Levi's thinking about? He did say that one day he was going to marry me back when we were in Vegas. We were in bed. Does that even count?

Am I ready for it?

~

Levi

"You're welcome to stay," I say as Galena packs her things. My gut rolls.

We're in my bedroom. I hadn't anticipated this. I thought once Kevin moved out and her house was for sale, that meant we were a go. She only stayed here three days while her house was prepared for sale, but then once it went on the market, she decided to move back in. It makes no sense. She'll have to keep it pristine for potential home buyers. It's so much easier for her to stay with me. We've already had this argument, and she's set on going.

She gives me a quick glance before going back to packing. "I think it's best if I live on my own for a bit. I went from one relationship to the next, and I just need to be sure, you know?"

A lump of emotion lodges in my throat. "Sure about what?"

"That I'm not just, I don't know, using the good feelings with you to protect myself from feeling all the hurt. I went from jilted bride to a honeymoon with you. Except for a week, we've been together ever since."

I grab her hand and pull her to sit on the bed next to me. "I'm confused. I thought we had something good."

"We do. I just need to be sure about things."

I cup her cheek, and she closes her eyes, leaning into my hand. "I'm sure."

She pulls my hand from her face and holds my hand tightly. "This isn't the end. I want to keep seeing you. I just don't want to live together. Not until…"

"Until what?"

She shakes her head. "I need to live on my own for a bit. After I sell my house, I'll look for another one I can afford."

"In Summerdale?"

"If something comes up on the market, I guess. As long as I can find a house within commuting distance of work, then I'll be fine."

Desperation claws at me. She's pulling away when we finally have a clear path forward. No more messy domestic situation. "You could just move in with me after you sell. I've got plenty of space. Save your money for something else."

"But this is *your* place. I want something that I own. I grew up in a tiny cramped apartment with three generations of family. All I ever wanted was a house where I could spread out and have my own space. I'm finally in a place to do that."

I struggle to remain calm, to try to understand. "So you just want to be alone?"

"No, I want my own place."

"I've had my own place for a long time. It's not all it's cracked up to be. All problems have to be taken care of by you, and it can get lonely." *I never felt lonely until I was missing you.*

Just then Baxter props his head up on my leg in commiseration. I scratch him behind the ears, appreciating his loyalty. Sadie wanders in, following him like usual.

"How can you be lonely when you've got this guy?" she asks. "And Sadie girl." Sadie bounds over to Galena and jumps on her lap. Galena hugs her and pets her.

"Right."

She looks at me around Sadie. "Besides, you said you're signing up for a film class in the city. You've got a new adventure in front of you, a new path."

"It's just one class. I was thinking about doing a documentary on the animal shelter in town and Best Friends Care. It could be an example for other animal shelters. It was all done by community fundraising and the efforts of a caring vet."

"And don't forget miracle worker Harper."

"Yeah." But Harper's magic still didn't fix me and Galena in the end. From day one, I've been into her, and she's been waffling on me.

She sets Sadie down. "Okay, I'm going home, but come over for dinner tonight."

I press my lips together. "Do I get to spend the night, or does that get in the way of you living alone?"

She completely misses my sarcasm. "You can't spend the night. You have two dogs to take care of."

"I could bring them with me."

"I guess," she says flatly.

She sounds so unenthusiastic about me making myself at home at her place my temper gets the better of me. I lift my palms. "Forget it."

"What do you mean exactly? No dinner?"

"I mean I'm tired of waiting for you to decide if I'm good enough."

"You are good enough. I just need—"

"Time," I finish for her.

"And space."

"Take all you need. I can't promise to be here when you finally decide I'm worth it."

She sits next to me and leans against my side. "It's not like that. This has nothing to do with you."

"Sure feels that way." I stand. "I'm taking the dogs for a walk. I'll see you around town. Baxter, Sadie, walk."

The dogs rush through the door ahead of me, excited. My chest aches, but I refuse to turn around. Even when I hear a soft sob.

I just can't be second fiddle anymore to her ex baggage. It hurts too much.

Now what am I going to do with this engagement ring?

19

Galena

So it turns out living alone isn't all it's cracked up to be. And it's not even the fact that I have an entire house to myself. My life feels empty because I lost love. Three days into my newfound independence, I realized not only was the love I felt for Kevin nowhere near what I feel for Levi, I'm starting to wonder if what Kevin and I had was simply a best friends-roommate situation. There was no passion, no strong feelings high or low, and definitely no excitement over a future together. It was just comfortable. I have to win Levi back, and with Kayla's help, I have a plan.

Is it a smart plan? Uh, maybe? Or it could be the worst idea of my life.

I tug the little red dress down again as I get out of my car. It's a new dress and a little shorter than I'm used to. The tugging is necessary because I'm not wearing anything underneath it. Kayla insisted I need to seduce Levi and then wallop him with my declaration of love. It's the only way to get past his defenses, which are fully up against me. I've seen him at the lake twice, walking his dogs. He was cordial and polite just like he is to everyone else in town.

I blow out a breath and ring the bell at Levi's house.

Arrooo! Arf! Arf! Arf! At least I know Baxter and Sadie set off the alarm that someone's at the door.

I glance around, making sure no neighbors will witness my seduction. I may just throw myself at him. It's the first week of September and just starting to cool off from the heat of summer. I glance down at my chest, hoping my nipples aren't poking forward visibly since I ditched the bra. So far so good.

The door opens to a stunningly beautiful young woman with long brown hair wearing a halter top and tiny denim shorts. *Crap.* Levi moved on. It's only been three days, but this is what happens. You throw a catch back in the water, and someone else scoops him up. My sister warned me I shouldn't wait too long on a guy like Levi.

"Can I help you?" the woman asks.

"Uh..." My feet are rooted in place even as my mind screams for me to leave.

"Who is it?" Levi appears from just over her shoulder, shirtless with a towel around his shoulders. At least he's wearing jeans.

"Never mind," I squeak, turn tail and walk as quickly as Kayla's stilettos will allow.

"Galena, wait!"

I wave over my shoulder. "I see you're busy."

I hustle around to the driver's side of my car and yank the door open. Strong arms wrap around me from behind. I'm too humiliated to fight. I just stand there, biting my lower lip and trying not to cry.

"That's a pretty dress you're wearing," Levi says by my ear.

"Thank you," I say stiffly.

He pushes the car door closed with his foot, keeping his hold on me. "Why did you run off?"

I try an experimental twist, and he loosens his hold on me enough to let me face him. "You seem busy."

He pushes his wet hair back. "I just got out of the shower after a run. I needed to clear my head."

I glance over toward his house and see his new girlfriend watching us through the front window. "You should probably get back to your girlfriend."

He glances back and gestures her away from the window.

She appears on the front porch and crosses her arms. "Rude."

He sighs and drops his head.

She marches over to us, and for a moment I'm not sure if she's going to slap me or Levi. Instead she pokes him in the side. "Introduce me to your girlfriend."

"We broke up," I say, "three days ago, and I-I shouldn't have come. Excuse me." I try to open my car door, but Levi's hand keeps it closed.

"Galena, this is Avery, my sister. She's visiting while her husband is deployed."

I look from Avery to Levi and back again. Similar coloring, but otherwise they don't look alike. Avery has high cheekbones, a long thin nose, and full lips. Levi has a wider nose that turns up a little at the end, narrower lips. I guess he could have high cheekbones under that beard.

I tug my dress down again, trying in vain to make it longer.

"We were going to The Horseman Inn for lunch," Levi says. "You want to join us?"

I immediately imagine sitting bare-bottomed on a chair at the restaurant or, worse, a bar stool where the dress will surely ride up and show most of my leg, possibly my hip and ass too. "I can't."

"Of course you can," Avery says. "Besides, I want to get to know the woman who inspired big brother to—"

"Get another dog," Levi finishes for her. "Baxter needed a friend."

My brows scrunch together in confusion. That was Levi's idea. Something's up. Avery and Levi are having some kind of silent communication. She lifts her brows and shoots him a pointed look full of meaning I don't get. He seems to understand. Were they talking about me before I showed up for my grand seduction?

God, this is embarrassing. The one time I try to flaunt my sexuality and it's all mixed up with a public outing to a restaurant with his sister.

Sweat makes my glasses slip down my nose. Should've went with contacts for this! I push my glasses back in place. "Actually, I just stopped by to say hi. I'm heading next door to Kayla's for lunch."

"You wear a killer dress like that for lunch with a friend?" Avery asks.

Heat rises up my neck. "I should go."

Levi grabs my arm before I can make my escape. "I'll invite her and Adam too."

I subtly push his hand off my arm and debate getting in my car or walking next door to Kayla's house like that was the plan all along.

"Is there a problem?" Avery asks me.

I shake my head. "Nope. No problem. I'm just not very hungry after all. Nice meeting you."

She gives me a knowing look and backs away a few steps, gesturing for me to join her. I walk over just as a breeze picks up, forcing me to hold my dress down with both hands. My purse strap falls, hanging around my wrist and tangling with my leg, but I don't dare fix it.

"I think I know what's going on here," she says, smiling. "You need some alone time with Levi for a big talk about the relationship. Levi says there's nothing to talk about, but I've never seen him so down. It's no problem. I'll just grab lunch and bring something back for you both."

Kayla appears on her front porch and waves. "Hi, guys! We'd love to join you for lunch."

My head whips toward Levi, who's holding his phone. Apparently, he texted them. Adam appears a moment later on the porch with Kayla, and they walk next door to see us.

I look toward my car and back to the concerned face of Avery.

"You're not going to bail before your big talk, are you?" she asks quietly.

Kayla hugs me. "Love this little red dress. I told you it would work."

"I just got here," I say under my breath.

"You work fast!"

Levi cocks his head. "What's going on?"

"You guys need to talk," Avery says. "We'll grab lunch for you. Besides, I can catch up with Adam here and get to know Kayla better."

Before I can get out a word of protest, Kayla, suddenly realizing I haven't made any moves yet, links her arm in Avery's and guides her toward Kayla and Adam's driveway. "I'll drive," Kayla says. "Adam's told me about you. How do you like Germany?"

Levi's eyes are intent on mine. "Did you want to come in?"

I stare down at the little red dress that was supposed to do all the work for me. The grand seduction suddenly feels so far beyond my grasp. Since when have I ever been the sexy vixen who drives men wild enough to forget they're not happy with me at the moment?

"Sure," I say.

He walks to the door and holds it open for me. "Don't sound too excited."

I step inside, and the dogs rush me, jumping on my bare legs, their claws scraping down the sensitive skin. I jump around, lifting my legs away from them in a crazy dance. "Ouch, down!"

"Down," Levi orders and grabs them both by the collars, waiting for them to obey. They finally both lie down, and he lets go, rising slowly, his gaze trailing from my slightly reddened legs to my barely covered hips and then up, lingering on my breasts, bra-free, the nipples poking forward in the thin cotton. They like him. Finally, he meets my eyes.

"Galena, are you naked under that pretty dress?" His voice is husky.

I slap the dress. "Yes! I was supposed to seduce you out of being mad at me, and now I don't know what I was thinking."

His arm bands around my waist, pulling me close. "I'm not mad at you."

I rest my hands on his chest and feel his heart pounding as hard as my own. "You're not?"

He shakes his head.

"I wanted to make a grand gesture. Seduction followed by a declaration of my love."

He slides a hand down my spine, resting it on my lower back. "Don't let me stop you."

Welp, I'm in this far. I undo the back zipper and shimmy out of the dress. I step out of it. "I love you. I miss you."

His gaze eats me up from head to toe. When he speaks, he sounds out of breath. "God, you're beautiful."

I hold my breath, bared to him, my heart and body exposed. I may have ignited his lust, but what about the rest?

He frames my face with his hands and rests his forehead against mine. "I love you too. I'll always love you."

My throat clogs with emotion, tears leaking from my eyes. "I'm sorry it took me so long to trust you with my heart."

His eyes well. "Don't be sorry. You needed time. I was the one pushing too hard. I'm just so glad you came back."

"Naked too."

We laugh.

And then he scoops me up, cradled in his arms, and carries me upstairs for the seduction that didn't go the way I planned but worked just the same.

Love wins against the odds. I never would've calculated that outcome.

EPILOGUE

Three weeks later...

Levi

"Can you say that again?" I peer around the camera at Dr. Russo, our local veterinarian. "About how you determine which dogs will make good therapy dogs?"

We're in the waiting room of his veterinary practice, filming my first short documentary film. He obliges with just as much enthusiasm as the first time. I'm smiling behind my new video camcorder. I'm taking a film class in the city. For my first assignment, I decided to create a documentary about the cool stuff Dr. Russo is doing with the animal shelter here in town. I figure he can use it to run on repeat in his waiting room or when he goes to town events with adoptable animals. Who knows, maybe it'll get larger attention and inspire other animal shelters around the country.

Galena is here with me. It's the night before the Fall Harvest Festival, and we're helping Dr. Russo set up for the fundraiser tonight at The Horseman Inn. A lot of people have dropped off donations, which he stored in his office. Tonight's a silent auction for the donations, followed by a party. The shelter always needs more funds to care for the dogs and cats.

Tomorrow, he'll be manning a booth for the shelter with animals for adoption at the festival.

After a few more questions, which Dr. Russo obligingly answers, I say, "That's a wrap."

"'That's a wrap.' You sound so professional!" Galena says.

I kiss her. "It's important to get with the lingo."

"You were great too, Dr. Russo," she gushes. Galena tells me Dr. Russo is handsome enough to be on TV, which is *not* why I chose to film here, but she says it'll help. Apparently, blue eyes with brown hair and light olive skin are especially striking. He's around my age, not too old. Look at me, feeling young again. That deadline from Dad's early death no longer applies to me.

He flashes a smile. "You can call me Dominic or Dom. I know I haven't made much time for socializing, but I hope you'll both consider me a friend."

"Absolutely," I say.

Galena nods, her cheeks flushed. It's okay for her to have a crush as long as she comes home to me.

Dominic gestures for us to follow him. "To the pile. People in this town are very generous."

I put away my equipment while Galena goes with him. Her house is on the market and has already had some interest. She lives with me now, taking a chance on us. I've reassured her every way I know how. Tonight's the night I make it official.

When I arrive in his office, Galena and Dominic are walking out carrying large baskets wrapped in colorful cellophane with bows.

"Can you believe this?" Galena asks me. "I thought it was just going to be a bunch of random stuff. It's all themed gift baskets! Someone put a lot of work into this."

I grab four baskets and follow them to Dominic's animal shelter van. He'll put the crates of animals in here tomorrow. For now, it's piles of baskets.

Between the three of us, we make short work of it.

Dominic shuts the back of the van. "Thanks for your help. I'll meet you at The Horseman Inn."

"You got it," I say.

I unlock my car and open the door for Galena.

"Thank you," she says warmly.

"I saw you crushing on Dominic."

"I'm allowed to look. You said so."

I get in the driver's side. The moment I do, she grabs my head and pulls me in for a passionate kiss.

She pulls back to look at me. "You're the only one I'm hot for. Anyway, be glad he's so photogenic. I bet your first film wins awards. You should enter it in festivals."

A surge of affection has me kissing her again. "I love your faith in my abilities. I'm still new at this."

"You're a natural."

We smile at each other, something we do often. Everything's brighter with Galena in my life.

"I love you," we say at the same time and laugh.

I start the car and back out of the space.

"People are going to say we're one of those disgustingly cute couples," she says.

"I'm fine with that."

A short drive later, we pull into the parking lot of The Horseman Inn. Dominic's already here and left the van doors open, so we start gathering baskets to carry in right away.

Once everything is loaded inside, Dominic and I move tables to the perimeter of the room for the auction baskets. Just as we finish, two more volunteers arrive. It's Audrey and Evie Larsen, Jenna's younger sister. I haven't seen Evie in years, but she looks so much like Jenna it has to be her. The sisters are tall, thin blondes with sharp angular cheekbones and jaw. Evie's dirty blonde hair is cut short at her jawline. I bet she's in town to help with Jenna's baby. Jenna had a baby boy, Theo, last Sunday.

I cross to them. "Hey, Aud. Evie, good to see you. It's been a long time."

Evie cocks her head, studying me. "It's Eve now."

Audrey pipes up, "That's Levi Appleton, our mayor."

Eve's lips part in surprise. "I didn't recognize you at first with the beard. And mayor too."

"No one else wanted the job," I say.

Galena appears by my side. "He's a great mayor, and he's venturing into filmmaking too."

"This is my girlfriend, Galena," I say.

"Hi, Galena," Eve says warmly. "Interesting to hear you're getting into filmmaking. I write for a TV show. I got a week off to help Jenna with the baby."

"Audrey here's a writer too," I say.

"She told me about that," Eve says.

Audrey gives us a small smile. She doesn't like to talk much about her book because she's not ready to share it yet.

Dominic joins us. "More volunteers, I hope?"

Audrey gestures toward him like she's glad for the distraction. "Eve, meet Summerdale's most eligible bachelor."

Eve's brows shoot up over wide eyes. "Hi."

Dominic stares at her for a long moment before answering hoarsely, "Hi."

Have they met before? Dominic didn't grow up here, and Eve hasn't been here in a long time.

"What do you mean most eligible bachelor?" Galena asks Audrey. "I thought you were seeing each other."

Audrey's cheeks turn bright pink. Eve looks away.

Dominic glances at Eve before turning back to Galena. "Where did you hear that?"

Audrey answers for her. "Town gossip. Always someone pairing up someone. Ha-ha."

"Audrey and I are friends," Dominic says, locking eyes with Eve.

"Exactly," Audrey says with a nod.

"But Levi said…" Galena trails off as I squeeze her hand. Whatever happened, Audrey doesn't want to talk about it in front of Dominic. Sounds like some mixed signals. Either that or Audrey told a little white lie about Dominic asking her out for drinks. I wouldn't blame her. General Joan had her in her Cupid bow's sight at the time.

Eve blows out a breath, looking around the room. "Right. Okay. I'm here in Jenna's place, so put me to work."

Dominic gestures for them to follow him toward a large box of decorations and signs.

Galena whispers in my ear, "Did I say the wrong thing?"

I look back toward the group. Audrey's efficiently arranging baskets along the row of tables while Eve is pulling rolls of streamers from the box. And Dominic seems mesmerized by Eve.

"It's fine," I say. "I have a surprise for you back home."

She gives me a knowing smile. "I think I know what it is."

I wrap my arms around her and kiss her. "Not that."

She wraps her arms around my neck and smiles at me. "What could it be? It's not my birthday. Is it our anniversary?"

I nuzzle into her neck before whispering, "Our three-month anniversary was last week. Remember I got you roses, and you got me my favorite thing, which you're so good at."

She giggles. "Shh!"

"Hey, lovebirds," Dominic calls. "We've got it covered from here. You're officially off duty."

"You sure?" I ask.

"I'm sure. Thanks for your help."

"Bye!" Galena calls.

I wave bye, grab her hand, and we head out the door.

"Can I have a hint?" Galena asks once we're in the car.

"No."

"You didn't get another dog, did you? They'll outnumber us."

"No more dogs. Two energetic beagles is plenty."

"Can you imagine two energetic kids and two dogs?" she asks.

I smile widely and take her hand. "I can."

She smiles, looking out the window. "I know whatever it is, it'll be great. I have complete faith in you."

My chest puffs with pride. I've earned her trust. She told me I'm the first guy she really opened her heart to. That means a lot.

A short while later, I pull into my garage and lead her into the house. The dogs greet us joyfully as if they haven't seen us in days instead of an hour. Galena gives them both some love and lets them out back. They bound right back in, eager to be with her. Galena's a woman with a lot of love to give.

"Meet me upstairs in five minutes," I say.

"I knew it," she says with a laugh.

Galena

Not that I'm complaining, but Levi's surprises are often of the sexy variety. It's fantastic, especially after my lackluster love life with my ex. Kevin's back to work at the lab and commuting to the city every weekend for a passionate affair with Iris from the wardrobe department of Harper's film. I'm happy for him. We both settled for comfort with each other. We were more like best friends who lived together when what we really needed was a lover and partner.

I undo my bra and slip it out from under my V-neck sweater, tossing it on the sofa. Hmm…wouldn't it be a sexy surprise to show up naked upstairs when Levi calls me? He's probably lighting candles and putting on some bass-thumping music. He knows I like that deep bass beat. So sexy. I kick my shoes off. I'm going for it, tossing each item on the sofa.

Sweater off.

Jeans off and panties with them.

Socks too. *Wee!*

Uh-oh! The dogs leap after the socks, and I run to get them, but it's too late. Baxter and Sadie take off in opposite directions in a game of chase. I go after Sadie, who chews much more than Baxter, dashing around the kitchen table and into the dining room.

"All set," Levi calls. "Come on up!"

"Okay, dogs, you win this round." I'd rather have sexy time with Levi than save my socks.

I dash upstairs and come to a screeching halt in the hallway, my heart pounding against my rib cage. Levi's filming me!

I cover my breasts with one arm and make a fig leaf of my hand. "Levi!"

"Sorry!" He puts the camera down. "I didn't know you were naked."

"What are you doing?"

"I thought it would be cool to record the event. I have a tripod set up in the bedroom."

"For a sex tape?" I screech.

He chuckles. "Would you be into that?"

"No!"

"It's not a sex tape." He gives me a thorough once-over. "I love you naked."

I shoot him a dark look and turn to go back downstairs for my clothes. If he's dressed for whatever this is, I'm going to be dressed too. I make it two steps before a strong arm bands around my waist, pulling me back against him.

"Hold on," he says in a husky voice by my ear. That voice sounds promising.

I turn to face him just as he pulls off his long-sleeved cotton shirt and puts it on me instead. It's long enough to cover me like a nightgown.

He opens the door to our bedroom and gestures me in.

I step inside, and my hand flies to my mouth. It's beautiful in a gaudy Vegas way. There's a Welcome to Las Vegas banner hanging over the king-sized bed. Party decorations of poker chips, cards, and dice hang from the ceiling. There's even a bottle of champagne chilling in an ice bucket next to a platter of chocolate-covered strawberries.

I drop my hand. "It looks like a honeymoon suite!"

He goes to the nightstand and picks up a single rose,

handing it to me. "I thought it would be cool to recreate the first time we got together. It was special. Unique. Like you."

I breathe in the sweet scent of the rose, closing my eyes as I try to memorize everything about this moment. This incredibly caring man who always makes an effort to show me his love.

I open my eyes. "I love it."

Oh my God. Levi's on one knee, holding up a diamond engagement ring to me. I drop the rose, tears swimming in my eyes.

"Galena, I love you so much, now, always, and forever. You were the missing piece of my life. The perfect fit. Will you do me the honor of being my wife?"

"Yes," I choke out, tears streaming down my face. I dash at them. "I don't know why I'm crying. I'm so happy."

He slides the ring on my finger and rises, folding me into his strong arms. I snuggle into his chest, listening to the solid thump of his heart. My own heart hammers away, my knees weak as I slowly come to terms with this momentous event. After I moved in with him, we never talked about marriage, and part of me feared he didn't want to marry me anymore. Maybe it was my own fear of taking a chance on being a bride again.

I lift my head. "You'd better go through with the wedding."

He wipes my tears away with his thumbs. "Are you kidding me? I'd happily marry you tomorrow, but I have a feeling you'll want your family with you."

"Everyone will be so happy. They love you even though we lived together before marriage." My parents visited two weeks ago, and I was very up front in introducing everyone. I wouldn't let them ignore Levi the way they ignored Kevin. Levi is too precious to me.

He cups my jaw, his thumb stroking the side of my neck. "Full confession. I assured your parents I would be proposing as soon as I was sure you'd say yes."

I stare at him, shocked.

He gazes into my eyes with so much love I completely relax, warmth spreading through me. "It's true."

I hug him tight and then kiss him all over his face. His cheek curves into a smile against my lips.

"Anyway," he says, "I wanted to record this moment so we'd always remember it, but I'll never forget it. You've made me so happy."

Euphoria lifts me up in a floaty happy feeling. "I'll never forget it either. I love you so much."

"I love you too." He kisses me and nips my lower lip. "Now let's get back to naked Galena." He pulls his shirt off me and scoops me off the ground, heading for his bed.

"You're so good at the sexy *sweep me off my feet* stuff," I practically purr.

"It's us that's so good. We're meant for each other."

"The odds were so tiny with our bumpy start," I say with a smile as he sets me down on the bed.

He covers me and kisses me deeply. "I was never good at math."

I laugh and then get down to the serious business of loving the man meant for me.

Don't miss the next book in the series, *Racing*, where Dominic and Eve unexpectedly meet again after a one-night stand and try so hard not to fall in love.

What if your one-night stand is your one true love?
Eve

I'm not one for relationships. Yes, I have good reason. So a fling with an out-of-towner the day before I fly to Summerdale, Connecticut, to visit my sister seems like the perfect no-strings situation.

Only my first night there, my sister talks me into attending a fundraiser, and there he is! Dominic the veterinarian (no last names given) lives *here* in Summerdale.

Can I survive an entire week of sizzling chemistry and his seductive looks? My only saving grace is that neither of us is looking for a relationship, and I have to go back to LA for my job in a TV writers' room.

But then the writers' union goes on strike, and my sister begs me to stay longer.

And there's Dominic tempting me for more.

There's no future for me here, and he's dedicated to his small-town veterinary practice. I'm not small town; he's not city. Yes, I should definitely go home. But I just can't bring myself to buy that ticket.

Sign up for my newsletter and never miss a new release! kyliegilmore.com/newsletter

ALSO BY KYLIE GILMORE

Unleashed Romance <<steamy romcoms with dogs!

Fetching (Book 1)

Dashing (Book 2)

Sporting (Book 3)

Toying (Book 4)

Blazing (Book 5)

Chasing (Book 6)

Daring (Book 7)

Leading (Book 8)

Racing (Book 9)

Loving (Book 10)

The Clover Park Series <<brothers who put family first!

The Opposite of Wild (Book 1)

Daisy Does It All (Book 2)

Bad Taste in Men (Book 3)

Kissing Santa (Book 4)

Restless Harmony (Book 5)

Not My Romeo (Book 6)

Rev Me Up (Book 7)

An Ambitious Engagement (Book 8)

Clutch Player (Book 9)

A Tempting Friendship (Book 10)

Clover Park Bride: Nico and Lily's Wedding

A Valentine's Day Gift (Book 11)

Maggie Meets Her Match (Book 12)

The Clover Park Charmers series <<sweet and sexy charmers!

Almost Over It (Book 1)

Almost Married (Book 2)

Almost Fate (Book 3)

Almost in Love (Book 4)

Almost Romance (Book 5)

Almost Hitched (Book 6)

Happy Endings Book Club Series <<the Campbell family and a romance book club collide!

Hidden Hollywood (Book 1)

Inviting Trouble (Book 2)

So Revealing (Book 3)

Formal Arrangement (Book 4)

Bad Boy Done Wrong (Book 5)

Mess With Me (Book 6)

Resisting Fate (Book 7)

Chance of Romance (Book 8)

Wicked Flirt (Book 9)

An Inconvenient Plan (Book 10)

A Happy Endings Wedding (Book 11)

The Rourkes Series <<swoonworthy princes and kickass princesses!

Royal Catch (Book 1)

Royal Hottie (Book 2)

Royal Darling (Book 3)

Royal Charmer (Book 4)

Royal Player (Book 5)

Royal Shark (Book 6)

Rogue Prince (Book 7)

Rogue Gentleman (Book 8)

Rogue Rascal (Book 9)

Rogue Angel (Book 10)

Rogue Devil (Book 11)

Rogue Beast (Book 12)

Check out my website for the most up-to-date list of my books:
kyliegilmore.com/books

ABOUT THE AUTHOR

Kylie Gilmore is the *USA Today* bestselling author of over fifty humorous contemporary romances. Her series include Unleashed Romance, the Rourkes, the Happy Endings Book Club, Clover Park, and Clover Park Charmers. With more than three million downloads of her books, readers all over the world love escaping into her hilarious feel-good romances featuring strong bonds with family, friends, and community.

Kylie lives in New York with her family, a demanding cat, and a nutso dog. When she's not writing, reading hot romance, or dutifully taking notes at writing conferences, you can find her happily crafting what will surely be future family heirlooms.

Sign up for Kylie's Newsletter and get a FREE book! kyliegilmore.com/newsletter

For text alerts on Kylie's new releases, text KYLIE to the number (888) 707-3025. (US only)

For more fun stuff check out Kylie's website https://www.kyliegilmore.com.

Thanks for reading *Leading.* I hope you enjoyed it. Would you like to know about new releases? You can sign up for my new release email list at kyliegilmore.com/newsletter. I promise not to clog your inbox! Only new release info, sales, and some fun giveaways.

I love to hear from readers! You can find me at:
kyliegilmore.com
Instagram.com/kyliegilmore
Facebook.com/KylieGilmoreToo
Twitter @KylieGilmoreToo

If you liked Levi and Galena's story, please leave a review on your favorite retailer's website or Goodreads. Thank you.